**"It's not too late to change y... ...d,"
Dean said. "I can turn around
and head for Fort Carson."**

"Can you please stop offering me the chance to change my mind?" Cara said. "My place is here." She almost added *with you*. But she didn't want him getting the wrong idea.

She felt a growing closeness between them, but they were totally at odds with each other. His world was one of knights in shining armor and damsels in distress. It was a world that she didn't belong in.

He glanced down at her with a solemn expression. "I wish you'd gone back to base," he whispered, "but it means a lot knowing that you want to stay with your commanding officer."

"I do," she whispered back, "I *need* to stay with you." She'd never been so sure of anything in her life. Her place was by Dean's side whatever the storm ahead. She touched his forearm. "We'll get through this. Don't worry."

His arm flexed beneath her touch and his body stiffened. "It's not me I'm worried about."

ELISABETH REES

was raised in the idyllic Welsh town of Hay-on-Wye, which is famous for its vast array of secondhand book stores. She grew up as one of four sisters, the daughters of the local parish vicar, and she spent much of her childhood reading historical romance novels. A love of romantic fiction stayed with her through her adult life and, after pursuing a very unfulfilling career in information technology, Elisabeth decided to try her hand at writing romance herself. Something clicked into place, and she now writes full-time from her home in Carmarthenshire, West Wales, where she lives with her husband and two children.

CAUGHT IN THE CROSSHAIRS

ELISABETH REES

⟨H⟩ HARLEQUIN® LOVE INSPIRED® SUSPENSE

Recycling programs
for this product may
not exist in your area.

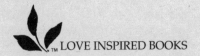

™ LOVE INSPIRED BOOKS

ISBN-13: 978-0-373-44610-0

CAUGHT IN THE CROSSHAIRS

This edition published by arrangement with Love Inspired Books.

® and TM are trademarks of Love Inspired Books, used under license.
Trademarks indicated with ® are registered in the United States Patent
and Trademark Office, the Canadian Intellectual Property Office and in
other countries.

www.Harlequin.com

Printed in U.S.A.

For it is with your heart that you believe
and are justified, and it is with your mouth
that you profess your faith and are saved.
—*Romans* 10:10

To David, Lloyd and Alys—
my wonderfully perfect family

ONE

Cara Hanson lay in the cool grass and lined up the target in her crosshairs.

The target was moving, searching for her, but she was invisible. Like a cat stalking its prey, she kept her weapon trained on the movement in the undergrowth. This would be an easy shot. She curled her finger around the trigger and smiled as she squeezed.

She heard the man cry out as he felt the impact on his back, and a deep, red stain appeared on his jacket. She'd got him! A cry of triumph left her lips, and she rose from the bracken like a monster looming from a lair. Her ghillie suit was covered with camouflage netting, making it impossible to tell whether she was man, woman or yeti.

"Aw, man, these paintballs really sting." A U.S. Army private crawled out from the thick bushes and clambered to his feet. He turned to Cara standing on the hillside and shouted, "How did you do that? I didn't have a clue where you were."

"And you never will," she shouted back, laughing.

The private took off his jacket and laid it on the ground, shaking his head in amazement at the perfect shot, right between the shoulders, just below the head.

"Nice job," he called. "Thanks for not taking the head shot."

"It didn't seem fair to fill your ears with paint," she called back. "It never washes out."

She knelt to the ground and removed her standard-issue M24 sniper rifle from its tripod, laying it on the grass beside her.

"Well-done, Sergeant Hanson," said a voice in the distance. She looked up to see one of her commanding officers walking toward her. "Your accuracy never fails to astonish me."

She rose to her feet, saluting as she did so. "Thank you, sir."

"At ease, Sergeant."

Colonel Carter Gantry approached her with an outstretched hand. She gave hers and he shook it warmly.

"Time for me to come clean, Sergeant," he said, releasing her hand. "There's a reason for this prolonged target practice today."

The colonel extended his hand toward a tall, dark figure in the distance. She'd noticed him watching the hills while she carried out her shooting exercises; saw him continuously scanning the mountainside with binoculars, hoping to search her out. This type of training drill usually employed the use of two spotters. Colonel Gantry had taken the elevated position, but she had not recognized the second spotter on the ground. Turned out, she was about to meet him. He began to walk toward her, and she took the opportunity to observe him, noting his wide shoulders and smooth, confident stride. He was wearing black combat pants and a black T-shirt. The fabric of the shirt stretched against the muscles on his arms, and she suddenly felt diminutive in his presence. His face was weathered; he obviously spent a great deal of time outdoors, and the dark stubble added to his rugged exterior. She squinted against the sun. She couldn't see his eyes, but she could just make out dark curls extending beneath his green cap. She recognized the beret instantly. This was no ordinary soldier. Only a Special Forces soldier was permitted to wear the distinctive green beret.

"Sergeant Cara Hanson," said Colonel Gantry, as the mysterious man came into plain view, "I would like you to meet Captain Dean McGovern."

Cara brought her hand up in another salute, as she always did when facing a senior officer. The captain saluted and she stood at ease. She instantly felt uncomfortable when he began to look her up and down with an expression of surprise on his face. Her skin prickled with heat, and tiny beads of sweat ran down her back. She saw his deep, brown eyes assessing her, crinkles appearing at the edges as they caught the sun's glare.

He turned to Colonel Gantry. "*This* is the sniper I've been watching all day?"

The colonel laughed. "Don't let appearances deceive you, Captain McGovern. Sergeant Hanson may not look fierce but, as you've witnessed today, she could take you down with a clean shot any day of the week."

The captain rubbed his face with his hands. He led the colonel a few paces away from Cara and lowered his voice. "She isn't exactly what I was expecting." He cast a backward glance at her. "Special Ops isn't for the fainthearted. I need to be totally sure of her mental toughness."

The colonel put his hand on the captain's shoulder. "Dean, I've been asked to provide you with the absolute best sniper that the U.S. military has at its disposal. Sergeant Cara Hanson is that sniper. Don't underestimate her. She's one tough cookie."

Cara remained standing at ease on the hillside, her

knees buried in thick shrubbery. She had experienced this same kind of reaction many times since joining the army seven years ago. She was petite in stature with small, elfinlike features and she knew that she didn't strike an imposing figure among the other soldiers of her Bobcats regiment. After all, no one was scared of a woman who looked like a Disney princess. But when she stalked her prey through the lens of her rifle, she felt as tough as any of her male colleagues.

The two men approached her. Captain McGovern's face was unreadable as he came to stand directly in front of her, his vast shoulders casting an enormous shadow on the grass. She couldn't help but steal a glance at his face. She saw that his nose was crooked, broken at some point, maybe more than once. His gaze rested upon hers for the tiniest of moments, and she gave a small shiver at the intensity behind his eyes.

"Sergeant," he began, "U.S. Special Forces have been given credible information regarding an illegal weapons drop due to take place in a region not far from here. The weapons are destined for a major terrorist organization, who will use them to launch an imminent attack on U.S. soil. We must take out their main man. And fast. We need a sniper who can deliver." He brought his face inches from hers. His breath was sweet and warm. "You only get one shot."

She gave a small nod of the head. "Understood, sir."

A hint of a smile passed his lips. "You up to the job?"

"Absolutely, sir."

He took a step backward and gave her one final look up and down.

"Report to B wing, Fort Carson, tomorrow, 0900 hours. Tell them you're assigned to Operation Triton. Don't be late."

"Yes, sir."

She saluted, but he had already turned to stride back down the hill.

Colonel Gantry smiled at her. "Trust me, Sergeant. His bark is a lot worse than his bite."

Dean paced the briefing room where his men would soon assemble. *Correction,* he said in his head, *men and woman.* He opened Sergeant Hanson's personnel file on the desk, despite having read it several times already. His admiration for her had increased considerably on reading that she had successfully taken out a suicide bomber in Baghdad, saving the lives of hundreds of civilians—an act for which she received the Army Commendation Medal.

He had been taken aback the previous day, seeing her skills for himself, the way she was so patient, waiting for the target to appear, her discipline in lying low, never once giving away her position. He had to admit that it was an impressive display of exquisite marksmanship. *If only she wasn't a woman,* he couldn't help thinking. He had no objection to women serving in the military; he just wasn't sure of his own ability to serve alongside them. His instinct was to protect women and shield them from danger. It was something he'd done during his entire teenage years, having continually guarded his mother and sister from his violent bully of a father. As he grew into a strong, muscled young man, he was able to use his own power to counteract that of his father's, but the image of his mother and sister cowering from yet another of his dad's drunken rages had been burned into his mind. By the time he was sixteen, he'd developed such a strong protective instinct that he knew his path lay in the military, serving those who needed defending the most. To wear the green beret was his one true desire, the ultimate symbol of male strength and prowess. Sergeant Hanson may be the best sniper for this job but, in his world, it was men who provided the safe havens. And the one person he wanted to place at the center of his safe haven at that moment was Cara Hanson herself. She had awakened feelings that he would need to guard against.

A knock on the open door broke through his thoughts. He closed the file and pushed it to one side, along with his feelings.

Cara Hanson stood in the doorway, her bright blue eyes staring straight ahead as she saluted.

"Sergeant Hanson, reporting for duty, sir."

He flicked his eyes over her body, which appeared even smaller in stature than the previous day. She looked very different without the ghillie suit and was wearing standard-issue fatigues. He was now able to see her face in its fullness, sun kissed and healthy. Her shiny blond hair was neatly tied in a ponytail, highlighting her high cheekbones and Cupid's-bow mouth. As a deep, primal emotion stirred within him, he wondered if he had made a grave mistake in allowing her to enter his perfectly ordered domain.

"At ease, Sergeant. Come in, take a seat."

Two more soldiers entered the room, and Dean rose purposefully.

"Sergeant Hanson, I would like you to meet Sergeants Gomez and Hicks. We'll be operating as a four-man team for this mission." He looked toward the two male sergeants, who were exchanging looks of surprise while shaking Cara's hand.

"Sergeant Hanson has been granted special dispensation to serve, on a one-off basis, as a combat sniper for this mission," he explained.

Female operatives were a rare species in Special Forces

and he knew she would be regarded with curiosity. Even he was curious about her but he knew that, within forty-eight hours, she would be back in her regiment and out of his life. *Keep it professional. Don't get too involved.* That was his mantra.

The soldiers took their seats, and Dean handed them a photograph of a man wearing the same distinctive green beret as each of the men in the room.

"This," he said, "is your target."

He heard a collective gasp from the room.

He raised his eyes to his team. "This is Major Christopher Moore from Tenth Special Forces Group. Twelve months ago, he infiltrated a terrorist cell in Ohio with the intention of supplying information back to the U.S. Government regarding intended targets. Six months ago he went rogue and disappeared from our radar. Intelligence has confirmed that he's turned against us and is now assisting the cell, helping them purchase illegal weapons and bomb-making equipment. In short, he's gone to the Dark Side."

Sergeant Hicks raised his hand. "How do we know this for certain, sir?"

"The terrorist cell in Ohio was raided three months ago by the military. Secret documents recovered there confirmed our worst fears. They state that Major Moore revealed himself as a spy and pledged his allegiance to the group." Dean walked to the desk at the front of the small, windowless room and placed the photograph on it. His shoulders dropped. "Major Moore used to be my commanding officer. We trained together. I would never have believed he could turn his back on the Green Berets, but there is no place for sentiment in this mission. He is a very dangerous and wily enemy. We've been trying to track him ever since the raid in Ohio, and we finally have our shot at taking him out."

Cara raised her hand.

"Yes, sergeant," he responded.

"Is termination the only option here?" she asked. "Could we not take him into custody?"

Dean sighed heavily. "Sergeant, if that was an option I would take it. Major Moore is a highly trained Special Forces soldier and won't come in without a fight. We know he'll be taking part in a weapons-smuggling operation tomorrow in the Four Corners region. These weapons are seriously powerful, capable of killing hundreds in one deadly swoop. We can't risk his escape. I'm afraid we have no choice."

He felt his chest tighten, and his heart heaved. He straightened his back. "It's always difficult when faced with a soldier who's turned his back on his country, but this man is no longer on our side. He is no longer a patriot. He is a terrorist, so let's put personal feelings to one side."

Easier said than done, he thought. Major Chris Moore had been his loyal friend as well as his commanding officer. He'd thought Chris was a man of honor, a man of integrity, a man of faith. But he'd been wrong, wrong to believe that God's plan would spare him the pain of facing his best friend as an enemy in combat. After months of prayer, he'd eventually reasoned that God had turned His back on him, and he would need to trust in his own judgment rather than wait for a Heavenly answer that would never come. He turned to his soldiers and drew a deep breath.

"We reconvene at 0600 tomorrow morning for Q&A. Read your brief, get some rest and prepare your minds."

His eyes scanned the three soldiers and came to rest on Cara. He watched her for a few seconds as she studied the photograph intently, her face betraying a sadness that she'd successfully locked tightly away from view. Her face was open, readable and it momentarily mesmerized him. She looked up and caught his eyes upon her, and he felt her gaze penetrating his shell to the tortured core within. He quickly looked away and walked purposefully from the room, creating a draft that caught the loose strands of hair falling around her cheeks.

Glancing back from the doorway, he wondered what thoughts were going through her head. They were revealed to him when he saw her finger trace the smile of the young soldier in the photograph, before she hung her head to her chest. In that moment he felt a kinship with her that he'd never experienced before.

Cara steadied her hands as she pulled camouflage netting over the small army jeep. She was nervous, more nervous than she had ever been. She reached into the neckline of her suit and took out the silver cross which she wore around her neck. She held it in her fingers for just a second before tucking it securely back inside.

"Sergeant, it was clear on the briefing that no form of jewelry is permitted on this mission. Dog tags only."

She looked over to Captain McGovern, who was staring at her sternly. The whites of his eyes shone against the black smears on his face. Yet beneath the tension on that face, his handsome features still clearly stood out. She tried not to notice but it was hard. She may be an elite sniper but she was still a woman.

"This necklace travels everywhere with me, sir. It never comes off."

She saw a fleeting softness in his eyes. "Very well, Sergeant, I'll turn a blind eye this time."

He turned to face his unit and all three soldiers lined

up, standing at ease before him. He looked at each of them. "Radio contact is limited to target identification and emergency protocol. We use call signs only. Gomez and Hicks, proceed as agreed. Hanson, you're with me. Let's roll."

The chirping sound of woodland birds echoed in Cara's ears as she followed in the captain's footsteps. He led her through thickets and streams, continuously looking behind to check her position. She started to relax. She loved the outdoors and moved through it like a quiet wind through the trees. It was where she was raised. Since she was ten years old, she'd been able to hit a tin can from five hundred yards with her dad's hunting rifle. Her father had taken her on regular hunting trips and she had never disappointed him. He proudly proclaimed to the world that his teenage daughter possessed an aim that far surpassed his own. Her mom playfully complained about being a "hunting widow," but she loved the fact that Cara and her dad were so close. It was a bond that could never be broken—except by death.

No, she pleaded in her head, *not now.* She pushed the picture from her mind—the image of her father lying cold and still at the edge of the lake, blood seeping into the water from his outstretched hand. That fate would not befall anyone else in her life. She'd made sure of it. She'd become the best of the best.

Dean stopped ahead of her and signaled for her to come closer.

"You okay?" he whispered into her ear. "This is where we go our separate ways."

She nodded.

"Let me check your earpiece," he said, brushing his hand across her face to rest on the speaker in her ear.

Her breathing quickened as he adjusted the small black device, securing it firmly in place. As he pulled his hand away, she felt rough, calloused skin on her smooth cheek.

"Ready?" he whispered.

"Ready," she replied. And she was. She was born ready.

She navigated easily to her designated position and began her routine of prayer. Her heart was heavy with the thought of taking out one of their own. She valued the sanctity of life and didn't take her job lightly, but she knew that taking just one life could save hundreds, maybe thousands. When she had been tasked with shooting a suicide bomber in Baghdad three years ago, she hadn't hesitated. She saw the crowded market, with women and children walking freely, and she'd pulled the trigger to take a clean shot. The choice was hers, but she trusted that God would understand her reasons—protecting the innocent would always be at the top of her agenda. She would do whatever it took to fulfill the promise to her father at his funeral, when she had resolved to dedicate the rest of her life to using her weapon to save as many lives as possible. She would atone for her fatal mistake seven years ago, and her father's death would not be in vain. Even if it meant a lifetime of shutting herself off emotionally, it was the price she must pay for redemption. A click in her ear took her to high alert. It was Captain McGovern using her call sign.

"Red Four. Truck approaching. Target identification imminent. Prepare."

Cara watched as a gray truck drove into the woodland clearing about a quarter mile away. It moved slowly, like a lumbering elephant, coming to rest partially covered by the branches of a low-lying tree. She aimed her rifle on the door of the truck as the face of her commanding officer settled on her mind. His safety was paramount on this mission and she would not let him down.

Suddenly, she saw movement: a glint in the hillside to her right. A finely honed instinct told her that this was a telescopic sight, another sniper playing the waiting game just like her. She scanned the hillside with her binoculars, trying to make out a figure, a shape, anything. There! She'd found him—someone lying in the undergrowth, unmoving but not well hidden. She traced the line of his sight with her binoculars. In the distance, lined up perfectly in his vision, was another figure, crouching down close to the clearing. Her heart began to hammer. She took out her radio.

"Red One, please raise your right hand."

Dean McGovern's reply was thick with anger. "Red Four, stand down, await target instructions."

"Commander, raise your right hand." She felt the panic rise in her voice. He must have heard it, too. He raised his hand. She gasped, realizing that the sniper in the hills had his weapon trained on her commanding officer. She spun her body around to face this new threat and breathed hard, lining him up in her sight. She gripped her radio.

"Commander, new threat detected. Move position."

"Give details, Red Four."

There was no time to explain as a shot rang out from the sniper in the hill. She took aim and fired her shot immediately. The figure scrambled to its feet and ran, stumbling into the darkness of the woods beyond. She lost vision on him within seconds.

More gunfire echoed in the valley below. Voices bounced through the air, chaotic and aggressive. Before she could react, a huge explosion rocked the hills, sending a vast fireball billowing into the air. She watched it rise like a demon into the inky sky. She couldn't catch her breath. She froze.

Captain Dean McGovern's voice snapped her back to attention as his words echoed, loud and strong, in her ear. "Red Team, abort, abort! Fall back and regroup!"

She picked up her rifle and ran.

Dean banged the steering wheel in frustration.

"What just happened back there?" he shouted.

He looked at Cara in the rearview mirror. She sat, hunched and breathless in the backseat with a look of deep shock on her face. The jeep raced along the lane, whipping up leaves and woodland debris as it gathered speed. Dusk was settling, and the sky gave off an eerie half light, illuminating the black hills into which they fled.

He quickly slammed on the brakes as he realized he'd reached his rendezvous point. "Where are they?" he shouted, looking around anxiously, searching the hills for any sign of danger. "Gomez and Hicks should be here."

In a flash, Sergeant Gomez darted out from the trees and ran toward the jeep. He looked like a rabbit caught in headlights. He was covered in mud and brushwood, but he kept his gun raised, pulled close to his body. Dean pushed open the door of the jeep. Gomez hurled himself onto the front seat, slamming the door behind him.

"Go!" he yelled.

"Hicks," Dean yelled back. "Where do we pick up Hicks?"

Silence.

"Gomez, you and Hicks were paired, where'd he go?"

The sergeant stared straight ahead. "He's gone, sir."

"Gone?"

"He was in the direct path of the explosion." Gomez's voice cracked. "I couldn't retrieve him."

Dean gripped the wheel tight. "You sure?"

"Yes, sir, absolutely sure."

Dean clenched his jaw and his breathing grew quick and strong. The tires squealed as he pressed the accelerator hard. "What on *earth* just happened there?"

He noticed Cara jump at the force of his shout.

Gomez sat back heavily in his seat, rubbing his face. He was pale. "The truck was packed with explosives. This was no weapons drop. There were two heavily armed militia soldiers in the front seats. They knew we were coming. This was a setup."

Dean banged the wheel again. "Someone set us up?"

"There was a sniper trained on you, sir," Cara said, clearly trying to control the tremor in her voice. "I scared him off with a shot, but he was trying to take you out."

"Did you get a good look, Sergeant?"

"No, he was too far away."

"Did you injure him?"

"I don't think so."

"So you missed?"

"No, sir, I was firing a warning shot. I wasn't trying to hit him."

Of course, he should've known. She never missed.

The jeep's small engine whined against the speed at which Dean drove. He had to think. He needed somewhere secret, secluded. There was just one place he knew, and he wouldn't feel safe until he got there.

He looked at Cara again through the rearview mirror.

"Sergeant Hanson, are you hurt?"

She rubbed her knee, wincing. It looked as if she'd fallen heavily through branches and thorns. Her face and hands were badly scratched.

"No, sir."

His eyes flicked between her and the road ahead.

"This mission just got messy. You're not trained for this kind of assignment, so it's my job to protect you. You stay close to me, and you do what I say, when I say, understood?"

"Yes, sir," she said.

He wasn't convinced of the sincerity behind her standard response.

"Until we find out who tipped off Major Moore, we trust no one."

Dean watched her closely through the mirror. She blinked slowly and seemed to be trying to steady her breathing. She took off her helmet and pulled the band from her hair, allowing it to fall loosely around her face. She put her head in her hands. He grew concerned.

"Sergeant Hanson, stay focused. I need to ditch this vehicle and acquire another. While I look for something suitable, why don't you lead us in prayer for Sergeant Hicks? He was a good soldier and a brave man. Let's honor him and the sacrifice he made for us today."

Cara lifted her head and gave him a weak smile. She closed her eyes and pressed her palms together. She managed to say a few words before she slumped sideways on her seat and his heart leaped into his mouth.

He willed the jeep to go faster, in a race against time to reach a place of safety where he could tend to her wounds, whatever they may be. He knew she must be in a serious condition to succumb to total defenselessness. She was too proud and strong to let her guard down so easily. He allowed his protective instincts to come to the fore, having decided that he would do everything in his power to steer her away from danger. He suspected that she might rail against his authority, but he was adamant that she would not come to harm—not now, not ever.

TWO

Cara tried to open her eyes but they were gritty and sore. She struggled to sit up as the room spun around her. Her vision was blurred, and her head swam with memories of running wildly through branches, feeling fiery heat on her back. She could see a small window with white drapes, drawn tight against the low-lying sun. She looked down at herself. She was wearing the Lycra pants and tee that she always wore underneath her ghillie suit. But who undressed her? She was lying on a large wooden bed with blankets, next to a pine dresser on which her rifle rested, neatly in pieces as if someone had been cleaning it.

She sat bolt upright. Captain McGovern! Had she failed him? She scrambled out of bed and promptly fell, with a thud, to the floor. The door flung open and someone rushed in, picking her up and sitting her back on the bed.

"Careful, Sergeant, you're not strong enough to be on your feet yet."

She focused her eyes on the face before her. Yes, it was Captain McGovern and he was safe.

"What happened?" she croaked.

"You went into anaphylactic shock," he said, pulling her legs up onto the bed and laying her back on the pillows. "You came into contact with poison ivy while in the woods. You suffered a severe reaction to it, I'm afraid. We almost lost you."

"Where…?" Her breathing was short and shallow. "Where are we?"

"We're in a cabin in Wyoming," he said. "It's my secret hideaway. No one knows about this place but me." He smiled at her. "And now you, of course."

She realized that this was the first time she'd seen him smile. His teeth were perfectly aligned, gleaming white against the olive hue of his skin. She saw a new gentleness in his face, and the memory of his firm, strong arms cradling her sweat-drenched body flashed into her mind. She hated being weak and out of control. But at least she didn't mess up. Not this time. She was grateful for that.

She lay back on the pillows. "How long have I been out?"

"About twelve hours. Luckily, I keep a well-stocked medicine box here in the cabin. We managed to get you here in time and administer adrenaline and antihistamines."

She raised her hand to her head and touched it gingerly. Everything felt puffy and swollen. Dean's face appeared over her, concern etched into the lines and furrows. He put his hand underneath her neck and raised her head up, bringing a cool drink of water to her lips. She sipped it gratefully, allowing the coldness of the liquid to soothe her tight throat.

He gently placed her head back on the pillow. "You should have disclosed your allergy to poison ivy when you enlisted," he said, unscrewing the top from a bottle of calamine lotion. "You must tell your superiors everything that might affect your ability to carry out a mission."

She closed her eyes. How could she tell him that she didn't want to divulge any frailty to the army? That she thought even a simple allergy was something she must hide from her commanding officers, along with any other imperfections in her past. She wanted him to have complete faith in her.

"I always carry an EpiPen," she said. "But I guess it wasn't enough to stop the attack from progressing. I know I should've told you about my allergy, but I'm normally very careful around poison ivy. I haven't had a reaction like this in over ten years."

She remembered being fourteen years old, straining to breathe, as her father carried her to the car to rush her to the hospital.

"It's lucky I found your EpiPen on the seat beside you," he said. "Is there anything else I should know about you? Any other allergies or weaknesses?"

He dabbed the lotion onto the blisters on her forehead. She realized that she must be puffed up like a balloon, and she didn't want him to see her this way.

"No, sir."

"You sure?"

"Yes, sir."

His gaze rested on hers as he attended to her wounds. He seemed to be searching her eyes for the truth. Could he see through the facade to the ugly reality that she had watched her father die before her very eyes? And that it was her fault. It was her greatest weakness, one that would stay with her for the rest of her life.

She remained silent as he soothed her soreness and washed up in the small sink in the corner.

"Where is Gomez?" she asked, thankful to change the subject.

"Gomez is here with us. We've conducted a debriefing session, trying to figure out what happened out there yesterday, but you may be able to shed more light on things. We just needed to get you strong again."

"Thank you, sir."

"Let's cut the formalities, shall we, Hanson? Call me Dean."

"Yes, sir."

She managed to laugh as weariness overcame her, and she couldn't fight the sleep that closed her swollen eyelids yet again. She watched Dean's face fade to a blur while she drifted into slumber, and she prayed that his life would not be in danger because of her weakness. As a sniper, she had guarded many lives, but no mission had ever made her feel this protective. She didn't know why, but she somehow felt connected with Dean, and she needed to recover so she could take her place by his side.

Dean stayed a little while as Cara slept, wanting to be sure that her breathing was steady and strong. She looked small and vulnerable, lying under the heavy woolen blankets. Looking at her face made him think of his mom, her eyes puffy and red after crying through the night. He pulled up the corner of the blanket and laid it over Cara's exposed shoulder, making sure she was warm and comfortable underneath. Even with her swollen features and crisscross scratches on her cheeks, she was still beautiful, and he didn't want to tear his gaze away from her.

He couldn't shake the feeling there was something she wasn't telling him. He knew that look in her eyes. He'd seen it too many times before. It was a haunted look that lingered behind the eyes of many soldiers in Special Forces—a look that said a thousand things about war and death.

As he watched her sleep, he wondered what she had seen to give her that same look. He thought he knew about all her combat experience from reading her dossier. *Unless,* he wondered. *This wasn't something she'd seen in war.*

Cara splashed cold water on her face from the white sink in the corner of her room. She was drained of energy, and she gripped the edge of the basin tightly to hold herself up. The sound of male voices drifted through the thin walls. Dean's voice was instantly recognizable, low and rumbling. She shivered. She was cold. And she was hungry. She pulled a blanket from the bed and wrapped it around her body, tucking it under her chin before opening the door of the bedroom and stepping out into the hall.

Her socks slid on the bare wooden floor as she padded down the hallway, heading for the light escaping from a crack under a door. As she approached, she heard the voices more clearly. Dean and Gomez were deep in conversation.

"All I'm saying is we have to be careful," said Gomez. "None of us in Tenth Group ever met this woman before, and as soon as she gets assigned to our mission, we get set up. It's quite a coincidence, don't you think?"

"I don't think Sergeant Hanson is a rat," said Dean. She heard his chair scrape on the floor and the sound of his heavy footsteps on the wooden boards. She flattened her back against the wall, hiding in the shadows. She heard the faucet running and the click of a kettle. She breathed out.

"Hanson says she had a chance to take out the sniper who took a shot at you," said Gomez. "Why'd she let him go, huh?"

"That wasn't part of the mission objective, Gomez. She followed protocol. You can't blame her for obeying the rules."

"It just doesn't add up, sir."

"Sergeant Hanson is a good, loyal soldier. I don't think

we have any reason to mistrust her, but she certainly will compromise our situation. She's not one of us. She's infantry, not Special Forces, and we'll have to keep her safe until we know what threat is out there. It's a problem we could do without right now."

Cara's head fell to her chest. *A problem?*

"Can't we just take her to the nearest base and leave her there?" asked Gomez.

"I need to know exactly what we're dealing with before any of us goes back to base. Moore has already terminated Sergeant Hicks. He may have his sights set on taking us all out, especially as he's got help on the inside."

"So what do we do now?"

She heard Dean sigh heavily. "We find out who we can trust before we go back in. We can't risk being set up again. I'll make contact with Fort Carson tomorrow. For now, we keep Hanson safe and make sure she's well enough to travel. I'll go check on her."

Cara froze in the hallway, eyes darting back and forth. She sprang forward and raced for her bedroom door, just managing to get her hand on the frame when the kitchen door opened, flooding the hallway with light.

"Hanson," called Dean. "You're awake."

"Yes, sir." She could not bring herself to call him by his first name. "I was just coming to find you."

He held the door open wide. "Come sit with us. You need to eat."

He ushered her toward the kitchen table, laden with used coffee cups and scribbled notes on pieces of paper. She sat, and a bowl of hot, chunky soup was placed in front of her. She ate eagerly, not bothering to look up or make conversation. She realized that she was famished.

When she had finished, Dean placed a mug of steaming coffee on the table and she warmed her hands on it, surprised at the way they trembled slightly.

Dean laid his hands on the table, palms down. He looked at her, unblinking, and she met his eyes, saying nothing, allowing the silence to sit uneasily between them. He seemed to be trying to read her emotions, but she did her best to give nothing away. The way he studied her face unnerved her, and she felt her guard slipping. He seemed rock solid and unshakeable, and in her debilitated state, she was irresistibly drawn to his strength. But it was a dangerous path to tread—she normally worked alone, depending on no one but herself. She couldn't allow that to change, no matter how much her attraction to him grew.

"Gomez and I have been piecing together all the information from last night's mission," he said, looking at her shaking hands. "Looks like someone on the inside tipped off Major Moore and he was able to plan an attack, hoping to take out our entire unit."

Her eyes flickered over to Gomez before asking, "Who?"

Dean shrugged his shoulders. "Operation Triton is top secret. Very few people know about it."

Gomez eyed Cara suspiciously. "What can you tell us about the sniper in the hills?" he said.

"Not much," said Cara. "He was a long way away."

Dean rested his arms on the table and leaned in her direction. "What was he wearing?"

"Looked like regular clothes—jeans, sweater." She cast her mind back. "And a red bandanna around his head. But no ghillie suit, no camouflage, no real attempt to hide properly."

"Not a trained sniper, then?" Dean offered.

Cara shook her head. "No trained sniper would be so sloppy."

Dean put his arms behind his head, his muscles flexing. "But his shot was good. He hit the ground right next to me. Another couple of feet and I'd be dead. It was certainly someone who can handle a rifle." He lowered his voice before adding, "Someone like Chris Moore."

He rose from the table and stood by the window. "Major Moore would like to see us all dead, I'm afraid. He's fighting a war against America and all military personnel are targets."

"With all due respect, sir," said Gomez. "We haven't been told anything about the terrorist organization that Moore is working for. Isn't that a bit odd?"

"It's highly classified," Dean said, turning to face them. "The military wants to keep it all under wraps."

Cara watched his face intently as it darkened. "We're in deep now," she said. "We need to know what we're dealing with."

Gomez shot her a sideways glance. "She's right," he said. "Whatever happens from here, we should know what we're fighting for."

Dean leaned back on the counter and looked between them for a few moments before speaking. "Do you remember the explosion that happened last year at Fort Bragg?"

Yeah," Cara said, "it was a faulty munitions batch. I read the memo about it."

Dean shook his head. "It wasn't faulty munitions that caused the explosion. It was a bomb, planted by someone who knew the base well. It totally blindsided us. A group called the United Free Army claimed responsibility shortly afterward. That's when we decided to put Moore undercover, infiltrate the UFA and shut it down from the inside."

"And they managed to turn him?" said Gomez, shaking his head. "If they can turn a man like Moore they gotta be strong. He's not a man who'd break easily."

"That's what I thought," said Dean, lowering his voice. "But they got to him somehow. Maybe he saw something in their ideology. Maybe he'd had enough of fighting in wars thousands of miles from home, wars that never seem to end…." His voice trailed off.

Cara looked up into his face, sensing the rawness of his pain. Just what had stolen his friend from him and left this wide, empty void? She voiced her thoughts.

"What exactly *is* their ideology, sir?"

Dean cleared his throat. "Their aim is to get the military to pull out of all overseas wars. They think the government is neglecting its own people to look after foreigners abroad. Until we withdraw troops from all overseas conflicts, the UFA says that every military installation and every serving soldier is a legitimate target. The bomb at Fort Bragg is just the first."

"How on earth did they infiltrate Fort Bragg?" Cara said. She'd only been there once, but it was the most heavily fortified base she'd seen in her life.

"Good question, Hanson," Dean said, raising his eyebrows. "They had a man on the inside but we don't know who. Truth is, we have no idea how many personnel they've turned. They actively target disgruntled and angry soldiers, usually ones fresh back from tours of Afghanistan, where they'd seen American soldiers caught up in roadside or suicide bombs." He closed his eyes. "Or worse."

Cara also closed her eyes, images flashing of things *she* had seen fitting this description. It was a subject that she knew bonded her and Dean together without question. Their experiences may not be shared, but they had a shared understanding, and no further words were needed.

"We don't know who the inside man at Fort Bragg was," Dean continued, "but we know he was angry enough to target his own colleagues. Four men died that day. We're fighting a war being waged by our own men and, what's worse, we don't even know who they are."

The three soldiers sat around the table in momentary silence as the enormity of Dean's words sank in. Cara knew all about fighting in far-off places, in hot, dusty lands miles away from her beloved home soil. She never imagined she would have to defend herself against her own countrymen. The news hit her like a brick, and she renewed her conviction to do all she could to prevent any more lives being lost.

Dean sat at the head of the table, his face solemn and still. "We must remain vigilant at all times because all of us are targets. Anything suspicious needs to be reported to me immediately, any time of the day or night. Understood?"

"Yes, sir," they said in unison.

"I reckon we'd all like a hot shower," he said, breaking into an unconvincing smile. "I'll check the cabin is secure while you two take advantage of the hot water."

Cara drained her coffee cup, noticing Gomez watching her from the corner of his eye. She stared at him defiantly, pulling her chin up high. He looked away and headed out the door, leaving her alone with Dean.

"How do you feel?" he asked, sitting in a chair next to her. He put his hand on top of hers. "Your swelling has subsided, but you're shaking a little."

"I'm fine," she said, moving her hand and placing it in her lap. "Thank you for everything you did for me, sir. I appreciate it."

"We have to trust each other, Hanson. And help each other."

"Gomez doesn't trust me."

Dean laughed. "Don't take it personally. Gomez trusts no one. He's a lone wolf."

She looked at her hands, clasped together on her knees. "I'm sorry that you feel it necessary to look after me. It's disappointing to find out I'm not accepted as one of the team."

A confused look fell over his face. He had grown more stubble since the start of the mission, and his face looked broader and darker.

She brought her face up to meet his. "I don't want to be a *problem*."

He narrowed his eyes as realization dawned.

"You were listening to my conversation with Gomez?"

"Yes."

He sighed. "Special Forces don't usually fight along-side regular infantry soldiers on these top-secret assignments. This mission has taken a very dangerous turn and, as your commanding officer, it's my job to keep you safe."

She lifted her head high. "Are you sure you want to keep me safe because I'm infantry and not because I'm a woman?"

He ran his hands through his hair. She knew it was a sign of frustration.

"Your mission brief was to terminate a target. Period. We didn't expect it to turn into guerrilla warfare. This is not your war, Hanson. This kind of dirty war is best left to the experts."

She decided she would read between the lines. "Best left to the men, you mean?"

His eyes locked on hers and he stared at her with such strength that she felt her toes curling.

"Don't start making assumptions about what I mean," he said defensively. "Your job is to take orders, not challenge them."

Her anger started to slowly simmer beneath her skin. She felt as if he were dismissing her, preventing her from playing her part in protecting those around her. She rose from the table and started to walk toward the door.

"I should know my place, huh?" she muttered under her breath.

Suddenly, he was there, in front of her, standing so close that his huge frame dwarfed her own. He was breathing hard. She saw his nostrils flare as his chest rose and fell.

"I am your commanding officer and insolence like that will not be tolerated," he said in a low, deep growl. "It is my job to guard your safety. Am I making myself understood?"

She said nothing.

"Sergeant," he said. "You will address me and answer my question."

She brought her heels together, snapped her hand into a salute and fixed her eyes on the wall.

"Yes, sir."

He didn't move while she maintained her salute. He was waiting for her gaze to shift to his, but it was resolutely trained on a spot on the wall—on a picture of a woodland scene. She imagined herself in the picture, taking aim on a tree far in the distance. She saw her father in her mind, encouraging her to trust in her skill and take the shot. For her seventh birthday, he'd bought her a small air rifle. She adored that rifle and, from that moment on, she spent hours practicing hitting tin cans off the wall in the meadow. Her dad nicknamed her "crack-shot Cara" and began to enter her into shooting competitions when she turned ten. She had a cabinet full of trophies at the family hunting cabin on the banks of Bear Lake in Utah. Her chest hurt as she thought of how she'd let him down.

She should have prevented it. She replayed the accident over and over in her mind, but the outcome was always the same. A bullet always took him from her. That would not happen to Dean.

Finally, he spoke. "At ease, Sergeant."

She stood at ease for a few seconds before turning on her heel and marching out the door. She left the kitchen and marched down the hallway, never missing a step until she reached her bedroom door and went inside. She then heard Dean leave the cabin, slamming the back door behind him. She sank to the floor and put her head in her hands. Keeping this man safe from harm was the biggest challenge she had faced yet.

Dean shone the flashlight into the outhouse, sending insects scuttling from its bright glare. He pulled his hooded sweatshirt up over his head, shielding himself against the rain that had begun to fall. He kicked at the grass as he walked, angry with himself for allowing his temper to flare. Cara didn't deserve to be treated like that. It wasn't her fault. The truth was, he just couldn't answer her question so it was easier to evade it, instead.

He couldn't stop the emotions that were stirring within him. His overwhelming desire was to protect this petite, beautiful soldier and deliver her back to base unharmed. He knew it was irrational. She was a fully trained, combat-ready member of the Fifth Infantry Regiment—the fierce "Bobcats." She didn't need his protection any more than Gomez did. She was strong and feisty, standing straight and confident before him, never flinching under his stare. She challenged everything he thought he knew about women.

He walked to the front of the cabin, to the yellow glow of light that was streaming from her bedroom. He imagined her inside, cleaning her rifle, carefully slotting each piece into place, before raising it to her cheek and lining up a target. She was the most determined and committed soldier he'd ever encountered, clearly driven by a need to prove herself. He should be commending her, not stifling her. Maybe she had a point; maybe he did treat her differently because she was a woman. He resolved to suppress this instinct to safeguard her. At least until she was back to fighting strength.

He turned his back to her window and stopped dead. The gate to the yard was wide-open. He knew he had checked it earlier that afternoon and it was firmly shut. He pulled his M9 pistol from his holster, flattening his back against the rough wood of the exterior wall and inching his way to the front door. It was a dark and rainy night, moonlight was scant and the movement of the trees in the wind could provide ample cover for any would-be assailant. He moved slowly and steadily around the cabin, his senses alert. The gate banged on its post, sending a thud echoing through the dark silence.

As he reached the front door, a noise caught his attention. He squinted into the darkness and saw a dark shape crouching in front of the rusty old truck parked to the side of the cabin. He'd acquired the vehicle in a hurry the previous day, knowing that the army jeep would be too easy a target to follow. One thing was certain: no sane person would try to steal this old jalopy.

The shape was moving. He suspected that, whoever he was, he was tampering with the engine, maybe even planting a bomb. As he assessed the outline of the figure, he realized that this was one huge guy, and he would never match his strength. He'd need Gomez's help for this.

He slipped quietly into the cabin. He found Gomez standing in the hallway with a look of concern on his face.

"I heard a noise," said Gomez. "I think there's some-one outside."

"Get your gun," Dean ordered, "and follow me."

The door of Cara's bedroom opened, and she stepped out into the hallway.

"Is there a threat?" she asked. He noticed that she had assembled her rifle and was holding it to her side.

"Go back inside, Hanson," Dean replied. "You're not strong enough yet. Let me and Gomez deal with this."

"But, sir…" she protested.

"No buts, Hanson," he barked. "Go back inside, lock your door and wait for us to come back."

She opened her mouth to speak and promptly closed it again. Turning her back, she went into her room and closed the door. He heard the lock click in place.

Gomez returned, holding his gun.

Dean's hand reached for the door handle. "Stay close, follow my lead and shoot only if absolutely necessary."

Gomez gave a quick nod of the head and raised his weapon. The door creaked open, and a gust of cold air blew through the cabin, creating a ghostly, high-pitched whine. Dean's heart was pumping fast as he put one foot out onto the wooden decking outside.

Whatever the danger, he would not let it infiltrate his safe haven.

THREE

The men stood together on the veranda, looking each other in the eye.

Dean gave a small nod of the head to Gomez, who nodded silently in reply. He mouthed the words *on three* and counted Gomez in with his fingers.

Dean leaped from the deck onto the wet, soggy ground.

"STOP! Hands in the air."

He aimed his gun at the dark shape hiding in the shadows of the car. It darted away, moving quicker than Dean thought possible. He looked over to Gomez, who was shaking his head in disbelief.

Both men gave chase, hurtling through the bracken behind the cabin, heading for the fields beyond. The black shadow scrambled over the fence and disappeared into the long grass. Dean followed the movement of the reeds and concentrated on the sound of rustling to follow its path.

"There," he shouted, springing over the fence and snaking through the foliage. Blades of wet grass whipped at his body, soaking him through.

They both moved like thieves in the night, wordlessly weaving through the field, tracking the sound and movement of their target. This guy was not going to get away.

Suddenly, to Dean's amazement, a huge, dark silhouette loomed from the grass sending a low, guttural growl in their direction. Gomez staggered backward and fell on his behind as the bear reared up.

"Stay where you are, Gomez," Dean said in a voice that was as quiet as he could manage. "Whatever you do, don't move."

The bear dropped to all four legs and stood before them, its eyes glinting in the darkness. Low rumbling noises emanated from huge jaws. Dean raised his weapon.

"Go on now," he said in a whisper. "We don't want any trouble with you."

The bear reared up again, sending another growl slicing through the air. Dean lifted his gun to the sky and fired a shot. It echoed through the night, reverberating for miles around. The bear dropped to his feet and fled. Dean saw its rough black fur shaking in the moonlight as it ran. In just a few seconds, it was gone. He turned to Gomez, offering him his hand. Gomez gripped it and Dean hauled him to his feet, laughing.

"Gee, that was a close call," Gomez said, clicking the safety on his gun.

Both men began to walk back to the cabin. Dean's face took on a serious look. "Let's hope no one reports it. We don't want anyone sniffing around, especially the police."

"I guess we gotta make sure we're more secure from now on," said Gomez, pointing to the wide-open gate in the distance. "That bear just walked right in."

They walked to the fence, and Dean closed the gate, making sure it firmly clicked into its latch.

"Do bears know how to open gates?" Gomez asked with a raised eyebrow.

"I don't think so," said Dean, squatting down and inspecting the flat patch of grassland in front of the cabin. "One thing's for sure, though. Bears don't wear shoes."

He examined the muddy ground, where boot prints were clearly visible, dotted all along the edge of the fence, like someone had been hiding under cover of the trees.

"Someone has been here," he said, feeling his heart begin to thud in his chest. He thought of Cara Hanson inside the cabin, weakened from anaphylaxis, totally dependent on his ability to provide a secure environment where she could recover. "Gomez, stand guard while I go fetch a lock and chain. Shoot on sight if you face hostile action from anyone or anything."

"Yes, sir."

Cara sipped her coffee at the breakfast table. She was still seething from the indignation of being locked in her room like a naughty child while Dean and Gomez dealt with the threat outside. How could she protect them from harm inside a locked room? She couldn't even bring herself to look Dean in the eye, lest she reignite the smoldering embers of their argument the previous day.

She felt physically stronger and more like her old self, although she desperately needed a change of clothes. She had worn the same stretch pants and T-shirt for the last two days. Dean had a full closet to cater for himself and Gomez but, of course, nothing fit her and she didn't want to highlight the differences between them by drawing attention to her need for another set of clothes. She would probably just have to make do.

Dean entered the kitchen. He had shaved. His face was smooth and she saw that his chin had a cleft right in the center. She'd never noticed it before. Despite her resentment toward him, she couldn't help but admit that his face was undeniably handsome with the kind of square jawline that made women look twice. She wondered if he had someone special waiting for him at home. A man this abrasive and uncompromising surely needed the presence of a woman to soothe his tortured mind.

"Good morning, Hanson," he said, sitting at the end of the table.

She said nothing.

"Ah, I'm getting the silent treatment, am I?" He poured himself a coffee. "I guessed I might, especially after our disagreement yesterday."

"I could have helped out there," she said, keeping her eyes fixed on the table. "I've encountered more bears than you could imagine. I would've known exactly what to do."

"I'm sure you would, Hanson," he said. "But I couldn't let you face any danger. I saw how much your hands shook yesterday. You were in no shape to handle a gun. It's not just your safety on the line out there, it's mine, as well, and I need you to be strong before you pick up your rifle again. I won't apologize for making the right call."

She let her head drop. He was right! Her hands had been shaking badly these last couple of days. She brought her hand up and held it in the air. It was reasonably steady, with just a hint of a tremble.

He leaned over to her. "Part of being a good soldier is knowing when to admit you're weak. You can't be strong all the time, so don't try to be."

She looked up into his face, momentarily dumbfounded by the way he'd just summed her up in a few words. She'd strived, for seven years, to be strong all the time, for her shot to be the truest, straightest and cleanest. It was the only control she had.

"Okay," she said quietly. "I admit that I may not have been ready to pick up my rifle again, but I'm better now."

He looked at her without speaking. She gripped her coffee cup tightly to control any tremor.

"I think we may have got off to a bit of a rocky start,"

he said, leaning back in his chair. "I've taken on board what you said to me last night, and I understand why you feel so passionately about proving yourself on this mission."

Her head jerked up. "You do?"

"Of course," he said knowingly. "Women in the military must have a tough time being accepted among their male counterparts. You probably feel like you have a lot to prove."

She nodded. "Yes, sir." He knew just the half of it.

He brought his chair a little closer. "But I am in command of this mission and I make the decisions. I know it may be hard for you to accept but I only have your best interests at heart."

She stared at him without blinking, realizing exactly what he meant. "You mean you want to protect me?"

She saw his chest rise and fall quickly. "Yes, Hanson, I do want to protect you."

"And *I* want to protect *you,*" she said, allowing the words to hang in the air for a while before adding, "I need to make sure that you don't walk into danger. I can keep you safe."

He looked taken aback as he nodded slowly, rubbing the back of his neck. "You're a superb sniper, Sergeant, there's no doubt about that. But you need to know when to take a step back. You won't always be strong enough to protect those around you."

She swallowed hard. His words cut open old wounds that she hoped were healing. She *was* strong. She had to be.

"I haven't failed so far," she said defiantly. "I've never missed a target since joining the military. Ever."

"But you will," he said quietly, as if trying to lessen

the impact of this harsh reality. "Eventually, we all miss something."

He looked into her face, holding eye contact for what seemed like an eternity. She stared back, feeling the unwelcome connection between them take a tighter hold. He seemed to know the inner secrets of her heart—the fears that she'd voiced to no one.

"Not me," she said, breaking her gaze away. "I won't miss again."

He opened his eyes wide. "Again?"

She shook her head vigorously. "I mean I won't miss a shot," she garbled, flustered. She gritted her teeth, angry with herself for revealing too much.

"Is there something you want to get off your chest, Hanson?" Dean said, leaning toward her.

"No," she said quickly, recovering her composure. She felt crowded. She pushed her chair back, away from his probing eyes.

She breathed deeply, reminding herself that she wasn't eighteen years old anymore, watching a huntsman lining up a shot on a deer. She wasn't on the hilltop, fumbling with her rifle, panicking as she took in the horror unfolding before her eyes. She wasn't still watching her father die from a single shot to the heart. She was here, as an elite sharpshooter, saving lives. She'd moved on.

She realized that Dean's hand had inched closer to hers on the table. His fingers were perilously close to touching hers, and she slid her hand from the table back into her lap.

"I *can* protect you, sir," she said. "I need to know that you'll give me a chance."

"I'll try, Hanson," he said, clenching his fingers into a ball. "But if we face any serious danger, I'll be the one standing on the front line. That's where I belong."

"It's where I belong, too," she said. "That's why you chose me for this mission, isn't it?"

"I chose you for this mission because it was a one-off job requiring your expert skills. I never anticipated it would get this complicated."

She felt her heart drop into her stomach. "Do you regret giving me the assignment?"

He said nothing. She looked away, clenching her teeth and pushing her hair behind her ears. It was obvious Dean didn't accept her as a front-line protector and she knew she couldn't change his mind. Not yet, anyway.

"You completed your mission flawlessly," he said finally. "Your skill saved me from an enemy sniper, and I want you to know how thankful I am. But I worry about what will happen from here on. We don't know what danger is waiting for us out there, and you're vulnerable to all kinds of attack."

"Don't worry about me," she said with conviction. "I can take care of myself."

His eyes flicked quickly over her slender frame and she watched him assessing her, no doubt wondering how she would defend herself against an assailant. She knew she was small and, physically, not powerful, but these things didn't matter to her. Sheer brute force was not a strength she coveted. A gun and a cool head were enough for her.

"You'll need a handgun in order to take care of yourself," he said. "Your rifle won't be suitable for close combat."

She nodded. She'd only ever experienced warfare from a distance—hidden away, safe and secure in the knowledge that she was invisible. The thought of facing the enemy at close quarters sent a cold shiver through her but she was determined not to show it. She knew she could handle it just as well as Dean.

"I keep a small store of handguns locked up in the basement," he said. "We should go find one that's suitable for you." He looked at her earnestly, betraying his fears for her. "I hope to God that you never need to use it but it's important we're prepared for every eventuality."

He rose from his seat, and she followed him to a locked door in the hallway that he opened with a key from his pocket. He flipped the light switch, and the bulb popped in the darkness. He clicked his tongue and extended his palm. "Take my hand," he said. "I'll lead you down the stairs until I can switch on the lamp at the bottom."

She took his hand and he gripped it tight, sending a jolt coursing through her. His fingers were warm and firm, and she couldn't help but feel reassured by his strong presence guiding her through the dark. Even when she was angry with him, she felt close to him, sensing that he was willing to bear the brunt of her fury with quiet acceptance.

He kept a firm grip until they reached the last step, and he was able to switch on a small, yellow light, casting a dingy glow in the windowless basement. He unlocked a steel-gray cabinet in the corner and took out two handguns.

"Let's try these for size," he said, handing a Glock 17 to her.

She took the gun from him and aimed at a spot on the wall, assessing the weapon's size and weight. She became aware of Dean's body behind her, his arms reaching around her torso, cupping his hands over hers and bringing his face to rest just to the side of her head. She caught her breath as goose bumps appeared on her skin.

"It's important that your grip feels natural," he whispered in her ear. "Not too heavy, not too large for your fingers. It should sit in your hands like it's meant to be there."

She watched his hands completely envelop hers until

they were almost invisible beneath his thick fingers. She felt smothered by him and pushed against his bulk. He stepped back, and she turned to face him.

"I have fired a gun before," she said incredulously. "This one feels perfect."

He put his hands in the air. "I apologize. I didn't mean to tread on your toes."

She found herself smiling. "By the time we're done on this mission, I suspect my toes will be bruised beyond recognition."

He laughed and leaned toward her face. "If that's the case, Sergeant Hanson, I'll be forced to carry you everywhere."

"Never," she said strongly, turning to help herself to ammunition from the cabinet. "I'd rather hobble."

Their laughter bounced off the walls in the dimly lit basement. She saw a sudden playfulness in his character, and she quickly felt the need to stop their closeness creeping further. She concentrated on her weapon, fixing a holster around her waist.

"Sir," she said. "There's something else I need."

"You got it."

She cast her eyes over her pants and T-shirt. "I can't wear these clothes every day."

"Of course," he said, shaking his head. "I hadn't realized. I'll take a trip to the nearest town and buy what you need."

"Can't I come with you?" she asked.

He rubbed his face. "I'd rather you stayed with Sergeant Gomez. It's safer."

She put her hand on her holster. "I *can* look after myself."

He looked at her and she stared back.

He bit his lip. "All right, we leave in five minutes."

* * *

Dean started up the rusty, old truck and drove out onto the narrow, winding lane, checking each direction thoroughly, before deciding it was safe. Cara was sitting in the seat beside him, wearing an old overcoat of his that swamped her petite frame. Her slim wrists poked out of the sleeves, rolled up several times. The truck rattled and bounced along the lane, heading for the busy highway in the distance.

He glanced over at her. Even in that old overcoat she possessed a beauty that floored him. He often had to stop himself from staring at her, studying the way her face rose and fell with emotions that she struggled to conceal. He'd caught Gomez gazing at her a couple of times but he'd brushed it off as "research" into his suspicions about her.

"Is there anyone you need to call?" he asked. "Anyone who'd be worried about you?"

"No," she answered quickly. "There's just my mom, but she's on vacation in Florida." She looked down in her lap before adding, "There's no one else."

"No one important in your life?" he asked, choosing his words carefully.

She turned her body to face his. "If you're talking about a boyfriend then the answer is no. My job isn't really compatible with dating." She looked into the distance. "I scare most men off."

He gave a small smile and nodded. "Strong women can sometimes scare a man."

She straightened her back. "Do I scare *you?*"

His lips curled into a playful smile. "Sometimes, yeah." It was a truthful answer. She *did* scare him but not in the way she imagined.

"Good," she said. "Then I must be doing something right."

He shook his head, laughing. "Gantry was right. You really are one tough cookie."

"Colonel Gantry was the person who recruited me into sniper school at Fort Bliss," she said, relaxing back in her seat. "If anyone knows me, it's Carter Gantry."

Dean decided not to mention that it was Colonel Gantry who persuaded him to take Cara into his team. He just couldn't shake his concerns about her suitability and had decided to recruit another sniper in her place. Colonel Gantry had insisted that Dean give her a chance. He'd followed the colonel's advice, despite it going against every instinct in his body.

"Gantry obviously sees something special in you," Dean said, remembering her amazing display in the Colorado Mountains. "He knows how hard you've worked to get where you are."

"When you put your mind to something, you can achieve anything," she said.

He glanced over at her. Her face shone with an expression he hadn't seen before. It intrigued him.

"I never met a woman like you before," he said, turning onto the highway, pressing the gas pedal hard to keep up with the fast-moving traffic. "You seem so…" He struggled to find the right words.

"…challenging?" she suggested.

He smiled. "I was going to say fearless."

"I guess you haven't met many different types of women, then," she said. "There are plenty of us fearless types in the military."

He mentally ran through the list of females in his life. It was a pitifully small number, mostly the wives of fellow soldiers, women he admired and respected, women he was fighting for. He thought of his mom and sister. They were good, strong women—survivors. But they'd needed his strength to save them. They couldn't have faced the terror of his father alone. They would certainly never have thought that *they* were capable of protecting *him*.

"I guess you're right, Hanson," he admitted. "I haven't met many different types of women." He stopped himself from adding that he hadn't actually met many women at all.

"What about you?" she asked suddenly, seeming to want to turn the spotlight on him. "Is there anyone in your life?"

He cracked his knuckles as he gripped the steering wheel tight. "My life is in Special Forces. Needless to say, I don't get out much."

"Maybe Gomez isn't the only lone wolf."

He forced a laugh. "I think we're all lone wolves in Special Forces. We've all got something driving us forward, pushing us to win every battle."

"What drives you?"

He glanced over at her. She looked expectantly at him, interested in his response. He began to feel uncomfortable and wished he'd chosen a different topic of conversation. He didn't want her probing into his personal life, trying to figure out what makes him tick.

"De oppresso liber," he said finally.

She looked quizzically at him.

"It's the Special Forces motto," he explained. "To liberate the oppressed. Freeing people from tyranny and despair is what drives me forward. It makes it all worthwhile."

He'd already experienced enough tyranny in his own life to know how suffocating it was, how it took hold of your life and sucked it dry. He was determined not to let it happen in any walk of life, just as he'd been determined to stop it happening in his own family. A bully was a bully, whatever language he spoke, and he would never stand by and watch the needy and vulnerable be beaten and broken.

"It's your own personal mission, huh?" she said, cutting a little too close to the bone for his liking.

He winced. "You could say that."

He felt her watching him closely as she spoke. "You ever thought you might want to settle down someday?"

He widened his eyes in surprise at the boldness of the question. This was definitely stepping outside his comfort zone.

"Like I said," he answered, keeping his eyes fixed on the road, "my life is in Special Forces."

She could read into that what she liked. She'd probed deep enough.

"While we're on the subject," he said, shifting in his seat, "is there a white picket fence in your future?"

"I doubt it," she said with a shrug. "I'm not the settling-down type. There aren't many men who'd accept me as a wife."

He raised his eyebrows. Was she kidding? He could think of a whole bunch of men who'd be glad to have her by their side. Not him, though. She and he were totally incompatible. That much was obvious.

"I'm sure there's some guy for you out there, Hanson," he said. "He'll find you."

"Yeah," she said, looking out the window. He couldn't be sure, but he thought he heard her mutter under her breath, "If he looks hard enough."

They drove in silence until he pulled into a small mall and parked in front of a store that read Darleen's Fashions.

Dean stepped out of the truck and went to open her door for her. He stopped himself, deciding to wait for her to join him, instead. The more distance he kept from her, the less chance there was of him treading on her toes.

Dean punched in a number at a pay phone. He knew he had to be careful, as this would be a nonsecure line, and he didn't want to advertise their presence to any unfriendly ears. Cara's shopping trip had already made him jumpy. He didn't like her being so visible in a public place, but, thankfully, she had known exactly what items she wanted and purchased them quickly. It came as no surprise to see that all her choices were functional and practical— exactly like her.

The receiver on the other end was snatched up on the first ring.

"Gantry here."

"Carter, it's Dean."

"Dean! Where are you?"

"I'd rather not say right now."

"We found your jeep. There was blood on a seat. Are you all safe?"

Dean was silent for a moment. "The blood is Hanson's but she's okay. Just scratches."

"What about Gomez and Hicks?"

Dean swallowed hard. "Hicks is gone. He took the full force of the explosion."

Colonel Gantry exhaled loudly. "We haven't totally cleared the bomb site yet. The media are all over us, wanting the full story. I'm sorry, Dean. I never knew this would happen."

Dean leaned against the pay-phone wall. "Make sure his family is looked after. Give them anything they need."

"I promise we'll do that, Dean. We really need to piece together what happened out there. You have to come back to base so you can debrief us. I can't say much on the phone, you know that. We need to talk in person."

"Carter, someone set us up. I don't know who, or what, is safe anymore."

"We know it was a setup. They were prepared, ready for you." Gantry took a deep breath. "I'm sorry to have to break this news to you, Dean, but intelligence suggests that *you* are the UFA's next target. You need round-the-clock protection."

Dean felt himself reeling in shock. "You know this for sure?"

"Yes, we know for sure."

He rested his forehead on the wall, letting the news sink in. *He* was the next target. He and Chris, once the best of friends had now turned bitter enemies, locked in a battle to the death.

He straightened up. "Can you guarantee that Fort Carson can provide total security?" He knew the answer to this question even as the words left his mouth. His base in Colorado Springs was well defended from outside attack, but the real danger was likely to be on the inside.

"You'll be a lot safer at Fort Carson than taking your chances alone," Gantry replied. "Wherever you are, you're vulnerable to another sniper attack."

Dean's senses sprang to attention. "How do you know about the sniper? No one from Red Team has debriefed you yet."

Silence.

"Goodbye, Carter." Dean placed the receiver firmly back in its cradle. Turning back toward the truck, he saw Cara's eyes trained on him as he stood on the sidewalk. He knew that her hand was resting on the Glock pistol, already loaded, on the seat beside her. This situation just got a whole lot messier than he ever anticipated. And Cara Hanson was caught in the crosshairs.

FOUR

Cara stood at the window, watching Dean pace the veranda. He had barely said two words since arriving back at the cabin. Whatever conversation he'd had on the phone, it had unsettled him. On his return to the truck, he'd been quiet and distant, locked away in his own thoughts. He was jumpy and she wanted to know why.

She opened the door a crack and his head jerked up, catching her eyes and holding them tight. He was under the shelter of the wooden canopy, standing far back from the edge of the deck.

"Dean," she said, stepping out onto the decking. "What's going on?"

It was the first time she'd called him anything other than "sir" or "commander." She hoped that he would respond to the familiarity of hearing his name, open up and let her in a little.

He leaped forward and snaked an arm around her middle, pulling her back through the doorway and into the kitchen.

"You shouldn't go outside," he said, releasing his grip. "It's not safe anymore. We found footprints yesterday. Moore may have found us."

She rubbed her belly, where his arm had squeezed her

tight, leaving a band of heat in its wake. She wasn't sure if her racing heart was caused by the suddenness of his movement or the shock from his touch.

Gomez appeared in the kitchen. He looked from Cara to Dean and back again, sensing the charged atmosphere between them.

"I checked every inch of the cabin, sir," he said. "I found no explosives."

Cara turned to Dean. She felt the Glock resting neatly against her hip bone where she had kept it securely holstered since Dean had given it to her.

"Footprints?" she questioned. "You should have told me earlier." She shook her head. "Are you deliberately keeping information from me?"

She folded her arms and waited for an answer, certain that he was still trying to protect her from the real dangers of their situation.

Dean ran a hand over his face. "Take a seat, Hanson," he said, pulling out a chair for her to sit. "We need to talk."

"I think we do," she replied, passing the seat along to Gomez. She took another chair and sat expectantly. If she stood any chance of protecting those around her, she needed to know everything that was going on.

Dean sat facing them and told them of the conversation he'd had with Colonel Gantry that morning.

Gomez was the first to react.

"I knew there was something fishy about Gantry," he said, shaking his head. "Man, I wish I could get my hands on him. I'd make him pay for what he did to Hicks."

"Hold on a minute," Cara said, leaning forward in her chair. "I know Carter Gantry. He's a good man."

Dean looked at her with an expression that was devoid of emotion. "When you've seen your best friend turn his back on his country, nothing is surprising anymore."

"Gantry isn't Moore," she said emphatically. Colonel Gantry had been like a father to her since her graduation from sniper school. He wouldn't betray them; she was certain of it.

Gomez swiveled on his chair. "If Gantry knows about the sniper in the hills then he's got inside information." His eyes came to rest on Cara's. "You and Gantry are good buddies from what I hear."

Cara met his stare. "Just spit it out, Gomez," she said, tired of his sniping.

Gomez rose from his chair. "Women never serve in Special Forces—never. But Gantry made sure *you* were on this mission. Why'd he do that, huh?"

Cara rose to face him. He was at least a foot taller than she was, but she held her head up high.

"Because I'm the best man for the job," she said defiantly.

She felt Dean's hand on her shoulder, pulling her back. His touch was firm but not overpowering. She stepped back and allowed him to place himself between her and Gomez.

"Let's all stay calm," he said, looking between his two subordinates. "If we're going to make it through this mission, we need to trust each other and work it out together."

"Agreed," said Cara, "but there's only one person who can tell us how Gantry got inside information and that's Gantry himself."

Dean turned to face her fully. "What would your suggestion be at this point, Sergeant Hanson?"

"I suggest we meet with him. It's our only option."

Gomez threw his hands up in the air. "No way! Gantry already betrayed us once. Why give him the chance to do it again?"

Cara ignored Gomez and continued to look at Dean.

"You didn't really give him an opportunity to explain himself on the phone. We can't just assume he's guilty without giving him a fair trial."

Dean clenched his jaw, and his face fell into deep thought. As she watched him, she noticed a single gray strand extending from his curly black hair and wondered if there was any truth in the tale that gray hair can spring up overnight. She couldn't imagine how hard this was for him to take in—a man he once admired and respected now wanted to put a bullet in him. She found herself wishing she could put her palm lightly on his chest to comfort him. She closed her eyes, quickly willing the image away. That was not how soldiers behaved. When she opened her eyes again, Dean was looking intently at her, as if he'd been able to read her thoughts.

Gomez jumped into the silence. "It's crazy," he said to Dean. "Don't give him another chance to terminate you."

Dean broke his gaze from Cara's and addressed Gomez. "I think Hanson's suggestion makes sense. We have to give Gantry the opportunity to defend himself."

Gomez shook his head. "Hanson is too close to Gantry," he said, turning away from her. "She's not objective."

"I just have a strong feeling that Colonel Gantry is someone we can trust," she interrupted.

"So we're trusting our *feelings* now, are we?" Gomez said, raising his voice. "You think we should just rely on your women's intuition to identify danger?"

"Call it what you like, Gomez," she said. "But I know Gantry and my gut says we can trust him."

"Yeah, well, my gut says he's a traitor." Gomez rubbed his neck where redness had started to creep.

Dean raised his head and took a deep breath, as if he'd made up his mind already. "Gantry has made it clear that he won't talk in detail on the phone," he said. "I'll have to meet him in person, but we shouldn't take any undue risks."

Gomez snorted. "It's one huge risk if you don't mind me saying, sir."

"It's a risk for me," Dean said. "You and Hanson don't need to take any part in it."

Cara jumped forward, her senses alert. "You're not seriously suggesting you go alone?"

"That's exactly what I'm suggesting," he replied. "I'm the one who's on their hit list. I'm the one who should be taking the risk."

"No!" Cara's voice rose higher than she'd intended. Dean looked at her in surprise.

"I won't let you do it," she said, feeling panic rise in her throat. "I won't stay here while you face this threat alone."

Dean looked at her with narrowed eyes, tilting his head slightly to one side. "And just how do you think you'll be able to stop me, Sergeant?"

Her mind raced with images of Dean, lying hurt and bleeding, defenseless and alone. She would not let that happen. But what could she do? She couldn't stop him physically. He could overpower her in a heartbeat.

She stood up straight and took a gulp of air.

"Sir, I'm the best asset you have in this situation. I can hide for hours, without a person ever knowing I'm there. Use me for cover, and I promise that no harm will come to any of us." She looked him squarely in the eye, feeling a strength of emotion leave her body and travel directly into him. "I won't let you down."

He fell silent, watching her face for some time. He took a step toward her.

"Are you fully recovered from the anaphylaxis?"

"Yes, sir."

She brought up her hand and held it midair. It was as steady as a rock.

He sighed, as if struggling with the decision. He rubbed his chin, where a stubbly shadow had already started to appear.

"Okay," he said finally. "You got your wish, Sergeant. We do this together."

She smiled. "Yes, sir."

Gomez shook his head and clicked his tongue. "I still have serious reservations about this, sir, but if you're determined to do it then count me in." He turned to Cara. "That was a pretty passionate argument you made there, Hanson. You got guts, I'll give you that."

She smiled and breathed a sigh of relief. *This* was what she did best. She knew that Dean would be safe in her hands and no harm would ever reach him. Not on her watch.

Dean checked the truck for signs of explosives, all the while keeping his eyes partially trained on the hills. He'd rigged up a makeshift cover from the door to the vehicle using blankets and sheets, providing some reassurance of protection from an enemy sniper. He'd worked in the dead of night, knowing he'd be safer from a bullet in the darkness. It wasn't exactly a professional job, but it was effective. He couldn't shake the feeling of being watched. He was sure that Moore was there, just biding his time, waiting for the opportunity to take his shot. He'd insisted on Cara remaining inside while he did all the outside work. It was his head on the block and he was the one who'd take the bullet.

He walked into the kitchen to find her preparing her rifle, meticulously checking each and every piece. She looked more relaxed than the previous day. He'd been surprised at her passion to accompany him when he asserted he'd meet Gantry alone. He really didn't want to place her in the danger zone, but her argument had been persuasive. Where Gomez was bullish and forceful, Cara was reasoned and composed. There was no doubt that her influence changed the dynamic of his team and it was for the good. She made him stop and think. She made him calmer. Was this why he felt so drawn to her lately? After so many anxious and sleepless nights, she was beginning to feel like a safe harbor.

"Are you sure you want to do this, Hanson?" he said, placing his hands on the table and bending to meet her eye. "It's not too late to back out."

She didn't look at him. She continued to assemble her rifle, narrowing her eyes in concentration, checking and rechecking each piece. When she'd finished, she placed it on the table and stood back with a look of pride on her face.

She then looked up at him. "Have you asked Gomez the same question?" She sounded irritated.

"No."

"Then why ask me?" she snapped.

He folded his arms. "This could be a very dangerous situation, Sergeant. We don't know what to expect and it's important that you're ready for it."

"You mean you want to check that I'm not scared." She lifted her face. "Am I right?"

He smiled without smiling. She was right. He *was* worried about her being afraid. He needed to know that she wasn't frightened of being hurt. He just couldn't help himself, despite all his best intentions.

"I didn't mean to offend you, Sergeant," he said, adopting a more formal and commanding tone. "My question certainly wasn't intended to cast doubt on your capability."

Her eyes never left his as she said, "It's vital that you trust my ability to protect you. We're a team here, right?"

He uncrossed his arms and leaned toward her on the table. "I have the utmost faith in your ability."

He knew full well that her aptitude for this job was second to none—he just needed to back off and let her prove it. And that was easier said than done. His mom had never been able to defend herself alone. He'd always been the one to step in and save her from the fear that dominated her life, even after his dad had long gone. The fear would never leave her. She slept with the lights on, even now.

Cara picked up her rifle and slotted it, carefully, into her black carry case. "And I have every faith in your ability, Dean. I think we work well together."

His heart quickened, just as it had done every time she used his first name. He liked the way it rolled off her tongue, as if she'd said it a thousand times before.

She hoisted the bag onto her shoulder. "Ready when you are."

He looked her up and down. She was wearing her sweatpants and sneakers, looking wholesome and fresh-faced, totally at odds with her steely interior. He breathed deeply. He longed to take her in his arms and shield her, using his own broad frame to guard her from danger. But he pushed those deeply ingrained instincts from his mind and stood before her as a commanding officer.

He put his hand on her shoulder. "Let's go."

Cara settled into the pose she'd adopted hundreds of times before. It was as comfortable as climbing into a warm bed. She was using the prone position, allowing for maximum support and accuracy. They had arrived two hours before the meet, so she could carry out some basic reconnaissance. She worked slowly, cautiously and methodically, scouting out the park, making sure there were no traps set for them. Even during reconnaissance she made sure she was undetectable. She sometimes felt like a shadow of a person, flitting unseen from place to place. She mostly worked alone. She preferred it that way, trusting in her own instinct and judgment. Her patience was limitless, and she knew of no other soldier who could match her endurance. She often wondered if being a woman gave her the edge over the enemy. Men often seemed impatient, unwilling to play the long waiting game, giving away their position too soon. Impatience meant death. In a war of nerves and concentration, she always emerged victorious.

She adjusted her earpiece and whispered into her radio. "Red Four in position."

Dean's voice floated into her ear, low and gentle. "Stand by, Red Four. Check in, Red Two."

Gomez reacted quickly. "Red Two in position."

She used her telescopic sight to gain visual on Gomez. He was her second pair of eyes, tucked away in the trees to her left. She bowed her head, silently remembering Red Three. She felt sure that Dean and Gomez were doing the same.

The park was still lush and green, in the mild Fall weather, with good foliage cover around the edges. Dean had chosen well. The meeting spot was in the wide open beside a large lake. There was little chance of him being ambushed here. The only danger was from a sharpshooter. And she had him covered in that respect, despite it being a little different than her normal working environment. She'd recently finished a tour of Afghanistan, where she'd provided cover for all kinds of operations, mostly protecting senior officers. She'd earned something of a reputation amongst the high ranks of the army, with officers specifically requesting her presence when placed in open and dangerous situations. Enemy snipers didn't stand a chance when she locked onto them.

Dean's voice returned to her ear. "Red One approaching destination. Communications blackout starts now."

She watched Dean walk slowly to the bench by the lake. He put his hands in his pockets and looked around as he walked, like a man out for an afternoon stroll. He sat on the bench and leaned forward on his knees, scanning the path for signs of Gantry. She lined him up in her sights, imagining how easy it would be to take him down, how fragile his body would be when pierced with a bullet. She was suddenly incredibly glad that she was there watching over him.

Then she saw Colonel Gantry appearing from the cover of the trees to her right. She recognized his tall, gangly frame as he strode down the path with a tense smile on his face. Dean walked toward him, still with his hands in his pockets. She knew that his loaded pistol was inside. The colonel extended his hand, but Dean shook his head and stayed well back.

The two men stood looking at each other for a few seconds before Gantry took a seat on the bench. Cara's crosshairs were perfectly lined up on the back of the colonel's head. He wore a blue baseball cap, pulled down low, as if trying to hide from her sight. She felt certain she wouldn't need to shoot but it was just a precaution. When it came to guarding Dean's life she couldn't afford to take any chances.

"You got a lot of explaining to do, Carter." Dean's face was full of resentment, sitting next to the man who he felt sure had betrayed him.

"Just calm down, Dean," said the colonel, raising his

palms to him. "Please listen to what I have to say before you make any judgments."

Dean craned his neck to look all around the park. "Are you alone?"

"You have my word."

Dean nodded.

"Besides which," said Gantry with a nervous laugh, "do you think I'd try anything stupid when Cara Hanson has got me in her sights?"

Dean's eyebrows shot up. How did he know about Hanson?

"Relax, Dean," he said with a wave of the hand. "I don't have a clue where she is. I never do. But I know she's here. You'd be a fool not to bring her."

Dean sucked in his cheeks. He almost had been a fool.

"She's my insurance policy," Dean said. "We've already lost one man. I don't want to lose any more."

Gantry's eyes softened. "I'm sorry, Dean. I know it hits you hard when you lose a soldier. I never saw it coming."

"Just what did you see coming, Carter?"

Gantry closed his eyes and took a deep breath. "I knew it was a setup."

Dean flew to his feet. "What? You knew we were walking into a trap?"

Gantry rose to stand next to Dean. "I couldn't tell you, Dean. I'm so sorry but I needed you to command this mission precisely because *you* were the intended target. The weapons drop was just a UFA rouse to get to you."

Dean took a step back, trying to catch his breath. "How do you know all this?"

"Two months ago we intercepted a coded telephone call between two known UFA leaders, discussing your command of Operation Triton. The gist of the conversation was that you are to be killed before you can get to

Major Moore. The UFA then deliberately leaked news of a fake weapons drop to us, so that we'd send you into the firing line."

Dean shook his head incredulously. "You mean you used me as bait?"

"Yes, Dean, I'm sorry but we did." Gantry tried to put his hand on Dean's shoulder but Dean shook it away. "We couldn't risk telling you. We don't know who to trust in Special Forces, and we had to ensure that you behaved normally. If the UFA had any clue we were onto them, they'd back out and we'd miss our only chance of capturing their highest commanders. Our whole plan would have been in jeopardy."

Dean threw his hands in the air. "You mean you had a plan? Because it looked like chaos from where I was standing."

A look of pain swept across the colonel's face, and he took off his cap, rubbing his forehead. "We had a second team on the ground, watching and waiting. We thought we'd be able to swoop in, neutralize the bomb and take their men into custody. We assumed we had all bases covered." He put his hands on the railings and looked out over the water. "We never saw the sniper coming. It set off a chain of events that was catastrophic. The bomb was detonated early and we lost our chance."

Dean swung around. "And I lost a man," he said angrily.

"It was never meant to end that way, Dean. You have to believe me."

Dean breathed heavily, trying to make sense of this new information. He knew he should be angry, knowing that he was sent into the firing line like a lamb to the slaughter, but he was a Special Forces soldier. He signed up for this. He knew that Gantry was telling the truth and had good reasons for doing what he did. Having a traitor on the inside totally changed the rules of play, and Gantry's gameplay had backfired. But he wasn't a threat. Cara had been right after all.

"I never believed your life was in danger, Dean," the colonel said with sincerity. "Why else do you think I persuaded you to take Cara Hanson into your unit? I knew she'd have your back."

Dean rubbed his face, imagining Cara watching them from afar, ready to spring to action at the first sign of danger. "Yeah, she did a good job."

"I knew she would," Gantry said. "She always does."

"But Moore got away," Dean said. "And I'm still at the top of his hit list."

"That's why you need to come back to base," Gantry said forcefully. "Look around you, Dean. There are hundreds of places for someone to hide. You're not safe in the civilian world. Come back to base, and we'll put you on lockdown until we find who did this."

"No way," Dean replied. "I'm not hiding away while others put their lives on the line for me." He ran his fingers through his hair. "Besides which, I think Moore has already found me."

Gantry widened his eyes. "Seriously? He found you already? Even we haven't managed to do that yet."

Dean gave a wry smile, remembering the superb tracking skills of his former best friend. If anyone knew where to start looking for him, it was Chris.

"Major Moore is an excellent soldier," he said. "He'll find me wherever I am. That's why I've decided not to run. If he wants to take me out, let him try. I'll face him like a man."

"That's exactly what I would expect from you, Captain," the colonel said, putting his hat back on, scanning the woodland at the edge of the park. "But it's not just your safety I need to ensure. You have an infantry soldier in your team that needs protecting from warfare she isn't trained for."

Dean looked into the distance. Cara was nowhere to be seen but he knew she was there, watching, waiting, praying. He pulled his radio from his pocket.

"Red Four, check in."

Cara replied instantly. "Red Four checking in. You okay?"

"Everything's fine, Red Four. There's someone here who needs to talk to you."

Dean handed the radio to Colonel Gantry. "Here," he said. "Persuade her to leave with you."

He closed his eyes as Gantry took the radio from his hands. He was torn between wanting Cara by his side and desperately needing to keep her safe. He massaged his chest where it had unexpectedly started to hurt.

Gantry spoke clearly and slowly into the radio. "Red Four, this mission is seriously compromised, and your safety cannot be guaranteed. My recommendation is that all remaining members of Red Team return to Fort Carson immediately. Am I making myself understood?"

There was silence on the other end of the radio.

Colonel Gantry looked at Dean with concern.

"She's fine," said Dean. "She likes to take her time to think."

Gantry tilted his head. "You've gotten to know her well, Dean."

"Unfortunately, I have," Dean muttered, turning to look over the lake. *Please God,* he said silently, *send her away from here.*

Her calm voice finally broke through the still air, floating to his ears above the birdsong from the trees. "I understand the situation. My choice is to remain with the Red Team commander."

Colonel Gantry sighed heavily and clicked his tongue. "This is not a request, Red Four. This is a direct order. You will return to Fort Carson with me. Today."

"I decline to obey that order, sir. My duty is with Red Commander and that is where I'll stay."

Colonel Gantry shook his head in disbelief and handed the radio back to Dean. "I never knew she was so damn stubborn. Her loyalty to you is commendable, if infuriating."

Dean nodded as the pain in his chest subsided. "She's an excellent soldier. I'm only just learning that."

Gantry adjusted his hat and turned to walk away. "I'll need to file a report about this. You know the implications of going AWOL but I won't seek your arrest. I'm on your side, Dean, always remember that." He smiled. "Let Cara know that I'm here for her anytime she decides to come back to base."

Dean nodded. "I'll look after her, I promise."

Gantry laughed heartily and raised his eyebrows. "I think you might find that she's the one who'll be looking after you."

FIVE

They drove in silence back to the cabin. Both Cara and Gomez had heard the entire conversation between Dean and Gantry transmitted over Dean's hidden microphone on his lapel. They said nothing, allowing him the opportunity to come to terms with the news that his own men had sent him into a trap. This mission had just taken on a new twist.

Cara knew she could be court-martialed for her decision to disobey orders. She also knew that she didn't regret it. This was a no-brainer for her; she would never leave Dean as long as he needed her. She was seated between him and Gomez, pressed tightly against his side. She fit perfectly in the alcove under his arm, which was stretched out on the wheel. She sensed his self-consciousness, so she tried to shift herself from the side of his torso, where her body naturally fell in the cramped space. His chest was firm and taut. She felt his muscles ripple beneath his shirt as he turned the wheel.

He cleared his throat.

"You took a big risk today, Hanson. You could get in serious trouble for this. It's not too late to change your mind, you know? I can turn around and head for Fort Carson."

"Can you please stop offering me the chance to change

my mind?" she said. "My place is here." She almost added *with you* but decided not to. She didn't want him getting the wrong idea. She felt a growing closeness between her and Dean, but their opinions were totally at odds with each other. His world was one of knights in shining armor and damsels in distress. It was a world that she didn't belong in.

He glanced down at her with a solemn expression. "I wish you'd gone with Gantry," he whispered, "but it means a lot knowing that you want to stay with me."

"I do," she whispered back. "I *need* to stay with you." It was true. She'd never been so sure of anything in her life. Her place was by Dean's side whatever the storm ahead.

He took a deep breath, as if suppressing a sadness within. She put her arm tentatively on his forearm.

"Don't worry, Dean," she said. "We'll get through this. Just wait and see."

His arm flexed beneath her touch and his body stiffened.

"It's not me I'm worried about," he said.

She took her hand off his arm, exasperated again. "Oh, please," she said, "we're not going to start on this again…."

"Hanson." Dean's voice cut her off.

"I thought we got past this…"

"Hanson!" He cut her off a second time. "Look sharp. I think we've got company."

She jerked her head to look behind, gaining visual on a large black SUV on their tail. The two men sitting in the front seats were difficult to see behind the smoky glass but she felt a menacing presence bearing down on them.

Gomez craned his neck to take a look. "We've got no chance of outrunning them in this rust bucket."

"In a game of cat and mouse," Dean said, quickly turning onto a quiet dirt track off the main road. "The only safe option is to be the cat."

Cara was one step ahead of him. She had pulled her rifle from her bag, already fully assembled and ready to go.

Dean glanced from her to the road and back again. "You think you can take out a tire?"

The truck bounced on the dirt track and smoke was billowing up from the tires. Visibility was poor and stability was even worse.

"I'll give it my best shot," she said. "Literally."

"Get down." Dean's voice pierced the air as a shot rang out.

Gomez ducked down into his seat. "They're shooting at us," he shouted, pulling his pistol from his holster.

Dean weaved the truck side to side across the track, trying to lessen the chances of a direct hit. He looked to be totally calm and in control but Cara wondered whether his heart was hammering as hard as hers.

"Gomez, break the window," Dean ordered.

Gomez sprang up and used the butt of his gun to deliver a quick blow to the glass behind their three seats. The toughened glass cracked and splintered. Gomez used his feet to kick the window free, managing to force it out in one whole piece. It clattered into the back of the truck.

Another shot was fired and she felt contact being made on metal. She would need to act fast to prevent this situation from ending badly. She closed her eyes for a split second and offered herself up to God, asking for His guidance.

She then turned on the seat, slid her rifle through the exposed window and used the frame as a stabilizing support. She knew that she would never be able to line up her shot with complete accuracy. The suspension on the truck was pretty awful and the speed at which they were traveling would make any shot a lucky guess. But she was their only line of defense and she would rise to the occasion. She bent her face down to the rifle to take aim, noticing a masked man leaning out of the passenger window, pointing a black handgun in their direction. She aimed for the front left tire. She fired. The shot hit the left headlight, making a "pop" sound above the drone of the truck's engine.

She shook her head and reloaded, instantly lining up for a second attempt. Then a bullet hit the edge of the window frame, just above her head. The sound of the ricochet sent her sprawling into the footwell. Dean's hand flew from the steering wheel onto her arm.

"Hanson," he shouted, "You okay? You hurt?"

She looked up at him and shook her head. His calm and controlled facade had dropped and she saw panic in his eyes for the first time. She used his arm for leverage and pulled herself back onto the seat.

"I'm okay," she said breathlessly.

"Gomez," said Dean, "Open fire. Provide cover for Hanson."

"No," she said, placing her rifle back on the window frame. "I can do this. Give me one more chance."

She controlled her breathing, took aim again and pulled the trigger. A loud bang reverberated through the air and pieces of rubber flew across the track. The SUV veered wildly before coming to a complete stop behind them.

Gomez gave a high-pitched holler and punched the air.

"Keep down," ordered Dean.

Shots continued to hit the back of the truck as they made their getaway. Only when they were well out of sight did Cara sit up straight and breathe a sigh of relief. She said a silent prayer of thanks before turning to face front, keeping her rifle gently rested on her lap. She wanted to keep it close.

"Well done, Hanson," Dean said.

She looked at him. He looked pale with dark circles emerging beneath his eyes. "You all right, Dean?" she asked.

"Yeah," he said, glancing in her direction. "I just thought we'd lost you back there."

She smiled. "Not a chance."

He turned his head to the side but not before she heard him whisper, "I hope not."

Dean felt himself jittery as he drove an alternate route back to the cabin. He wanted to avoid the highways and stick to the quiet country roads. He was acutely aware of Cara's warm body nestled into the side of his chest. It sent a spark through him and he tried to shift away, but in this small space, she kept returning to the nook under his arm. It was as if his body had been purposely made to fit her petite frame perfectly.

He was very grateful that she was unhurt. The shot that had sent her sprawling from the seat had almost made him lose control of the vehicle. Not because of the impact, but because he thought she'd been hit. Terror had gripped him. The relief he now felt having her sitting unharmed by his side was immense.

"We need to be constantly on our guard," he said. "Whoever wants me dead will stop at nothing until the job is done." He flicked his eyes over to Cara's hands curled tightly around the butt of her rifle. He marveled at how small and slender her fingers were but yet, how much power they could wield. They were so delicate and smooth, just like his mom's hands used to be. Two of Diane McGovern's fingers were now permanently damaged, gnarled and crooked from being slammed in a car door. They gave her constant pain in the cold of winter—a lasting reminder of what happened when she dared to disobey.

"Those guys looked highly organized," Cara said, moving her rifle to rest, barrel down, on the floor.

"They are," said Dean. "These terrorists are mostly ex-soldiers, trained for combat, just like us."

"Do you think they followed Colonel Gantry?" Gomez asked.

"Probably," Dean replied. "I don't think Gantry deliberately led them to us, but they'll be watching him. I should've been more careful."

He shook his head, angry with himself for not spotting the threat sooner.

Cara turned her head to his. "None of us noticed the car on our tail," she said. "Don't beat yourself up over it."

"Yeah," said a laughing Gomez, trying to lighten the mood. "Why beat yourself up when Hanson can do it for you."

Dean chuckled and looked at Cara, who playfully punched Gomez on the arm. He smiled, knowing that this gentle teasing from Gomez was the first step in his acceptance of her. It was how soldiers bonded.

He navigated carefully along the country roads back to the cabin, continually checking for signs of being followed. The wind whistled through the truck from the broken window. He needed to patch up the damage and carry on, something which seemed to symbolize the way he lived his life. Only when he was absolutely sure there was no danger did he turn onto the lane that led back to their temporary home.

Gomez hopped out of the truck, keeping his gun in his hand, and unlocked the gate. As the truck drove onto the gravel, Dean gasped.

He pointed at the door. "Someone has been here."

* * *

Cara looked sharply to the place where Dean was pointing. Sure enough, there was evidence of intrusion. Propped up against the front door, on the wood veranda, was a black book encased in clear plastic sheeting. She used her binoculars to magnify the words embossed on the front.

"It's a Bible," she said in amazement. "Someone has put a Bible by the door."

He breathed hard. "It's Chris."

She looked at him quizzically. "Why would Major Moore leave you a Bible?"

She noticed that he seemed reluctant to look at her, his hands pressed firmly on the steering wheel as if deep in melancholic thought.

"Chris and I used to go to the same church together," he said finally. "He knows this will get to me. He's taunting me."

"You used to go to church?" she asked, surprised.

He didn't have the chance to answer as Gomez rejoined them in the truck saying, "Looks like we've had a visit from missionaries."

"Let's not make any assumptions," said Dean, positioning the truck next to the makeshift cover he'd rigged up next to the veranda. "Be careful," he instructed. "We don't know who's been here so let's take it slow and steady. Follow my lead."

He exited the truck, swiftly followed by Cara and Gomez. Once under the safety of the veranda canopy, Dean picked up the Bible and unwrapped it from its plastic sheet. He turned the book over in his hands, rubbing his fingers on the black, dimpled leather. Cara watched the way he respectfully handled it, tracing the words *New American Standard Bible* with his forefinger.

He placed it back in the plastic bag and bound it tightly.

"We do a sweep of the cabin and perimeter," he said, holding the Bible at his right side. "Gomez, check the fences. Move quickly. Don't make yourself a target."

He turned to Cara. "Hanson, scan the hills for signs of someone watching us. I'll check the cabin."

With that, he dropped the Bible to the floor and took his gun from his holster. Cara looked at the book on the floor and resisted the urge to pick it up and place it on a ledge. She'd never been without a Bible for so long before and seeing this one lying on the floor made her realize how much she had missed her daily readings. She usually carried a small pocket Bible on longer assignments, discreetly slotted into her rucksack. She turned to the veranda fence, intending to retrieve the discarded Bible once her work was completed.

She set up her rifle on the deck and took out her binoculars to inspect the fields and hills in the distance. An enemy in hiding was no match for her finely tuned senses. Something would always eventually give them away— a bush that looks out of place, a flock of birds suddenly spooked or a glint in the leaves.

She methodically worked her way around the cabin, scouring the landscape. Then she saw something. She stopped and trained her sight on the shape in the distance. It was a small tent, well camouflaged but definitely a tent, just big enough for one man. There was no sign of any person or equipment. She felt uneasy.

She was glad to see Dean reappear on the veranda.

"All clear inside," he said. "Nothing looks out of place."

Cara told him of the tent in the distance and invited him to look through her binoculars.

His cheek twitched as his eyes fell upon the spot she'd identified. He handed the binoculars back to her and put a hand on her shoulder, guiding her away from the edge of the deck. "We need to go inside now," he said, taking a backward glance. "I don't want you out here any longer."

She turned to face him. "Do you think it's Major Moore?"

He moved position so that his body was between her and the hills. "There's no doubt in my mind that he's here. Make sure you remain out of sight. I'll go on a reconnaissance visit under the cover of darkness. Tonight."

She opened her mouth, but he brought his finger up to her face. It stopped just short of touching her lips.

"I go alone," he said. Something in his voice stopped her from arguing. She knew there was no point, not this time.

He opened the door and waited for her to go inside. She hesitated and turned to pick the Bible up from the floor. She saw that it was already gone.

Dean stirred his coffee slowly, his eyes resting on the black Bible lying on the kitchen counter. He wanted to pick it up, to smell it, to remember how it felt to be part of a spiritual family. But he didn't. He left it there, reminding him that he'd been a fool to ever believe in God's goodness in the first place.

He became aware of Cara's presence behind him. Even though she moved silently, like a cat, he always knew when she was close. Goose bumps appeared on his skin.

"Dean," she said quietly. "Do you want to talk about it?"

"Talk about what?" he said, keeping his back turned to her.

"The Bible. And why you think Moore left it for you to find."

He dropped his head. He really *didn't* want to talk about

it but, for reasons he couldn't explain, he found himself saying, "Chris and I used to attend the same church." An image of Chris standing, tall and proud, in the front row of their church in Colorado tore at his heart. "He was a good man—the best."

He heard her pulling out a chair and sitting on it. "I never knew you went to church."

"I used to."

"You stopped?"

He took a deep breath and exhaled slowly. "Once Chris defected to the terrorists, I didn't see the point in going to church anymore. If a man like Chris can lose his faith, what chance do the rest of us have?"

His hand hovered over the tightly bound Bible next to him. He balled his fingers into a fist and placed it next to his coffee. His stomach felt knotted and sick.

"I think the Bible is meant as a warning," he said. "Chris is playing some kind of game, taunting me. He's watching us, I'm sure of it."

"Have you thought that maybe it's God who is trying to reach you?" she said softly.

"No. God and I kind of parted company."

He turned around and looked at her, instantly regretting it. The kindness in her eyes was exactly what he didn't need right now. He needed to be alone, to harden his heart again and remind himself that Chris Moore must die to protect the innocent. He certainly didn't need the gentle probing of a woman, unpicking all the hard work he'd done over the last six months.

"Okay," she said, surprising him by backing off. "Well, why don't I look after it for you?" She pointed to the Bible on the counter. "Just in case you need it."

He picked it up and handed it to her. "Sure, but I don't think I'll need it."

She unwrapped the book from its plastic, and he watched her smooth the curled edges where damp had seeped in. She opened the cover page, and a piece of paper fell out, fluttering in the air before gliding gently to the floor. They looked at each other, silently conveying thoughts of trepidation at the significance of what they had almost missed.

He stooped to pick it up, turning it over in his fingers. On one side was black, scrawled handwriting that looked familiar to him. He sat at the table as Cara looked between him and the paper in his hand.

"It's a Bible verse," he said, feeling disappointment settle. "Just a Bible verse."

"Which one?" she asked, leaning forward, clearly intrigued.

He slid the paper to her side of the table and she read aloud, *"Ezekiel 3:17."*

She opened the Bible and flicked through the pages until she reached the right sheet. She read it slowly and clearly.

"I have made you a watchman for the house of Israel, whenever you hear a word from my mouth, warn them from me." She looked into his face. "What does it mean?"

He shook his head, dumbfounded. "I have no idea."

She looked down at the verse again before returning her gaze to his face. "Do you think it's a message, a warning of something about to happen?"

He reread the words, his eyes coming to rest on the phrase *warn them from me.* "I don't know anyone who would send a message like this," he said.

"Yes, you do."

His eyes shot to hers. She took his hand in hers, and he felt the warmth from her fingers permeating the chill that had invaded his body.

He pulled his hand away. "Chris."

"Why would he send this?" she probed. "Could he be trying to help us?"

"I doubt it," Dean said. "It's more likely to be a trap, something to draw us in before he attacks. Don't trust it." He snapped the Bible closed and pushed it to the side of the table.

As he drew his hand away from the book, Cara reached out and caught his fingers again. This time, he didn't pull away. He allowed her to cup both his hands in hers and remain there as they sat in silence, communicating wordlessly. He hated the fact that she knew how he felt, picking at an old wound that simply refused to heal. He was determined to bind his pain up tight this time and never allow anyone to expose a chink in his armor, no matter what.

Gomez appeared in the kitchen doorway, assessing the scene in front of him. "Am I interrupting something?" he said with a laugh.

Dean quickly withdrew his hands and placed them around his coffee mug, pulling up the shutters once again. He decided that he wouldn't tell Gomez about the Bible verse. He knew it had been intended for him alone, and only he could interpret it. He looked at Cara sitting opposite him, perfectly calm and serene, and he cast his gaze away as an awful sense of foreboding gripped his heart.

Cara shook her head, feeling tired and groggy. She looked at the clock: 8:00 a.m. She'd slept later than she'd intended. She and Gomez had taken turns guarding the cabin through the night. Her last shift had finished just as Dean was preparing to leave on his reconnaissance mission to the tent in the hills. She'd watched his tall frame head out into the blackness, and she kept him in her sights until darkness shrouded him from view. She'd swallowed her worry and turned her attentions to ensuring that she and Gomez remained safe until his return. She knew that Dean needed some time alone—time to order his mind and reflect on all that had happened. Time also, perhaps, to pray?

She roused herself from her bed and quickly showered and dressed. The Bible that had been left for them the previous day was sitting on her dresser. She was glad to have it. It felt like an old friend.

She holstered her gun and said a quick prayer for the day. A voice cut through her offerings, bringing her sharply back into reality. It was Dean, his voice loud and panicked.

"Hanson, Hanson. Where are you?"

She ran from her room to find him in the hallway, eyes wide and alert. He looked relieved to see her.

"Come quickly," he said breathlessly, "and bring the Bible."

She ran back and snatched the Bible from her dresser before following him into the kitchen. Sitting on the floor of the kitchen was Gomez, wincing and rubbing the back of his head.

"Moore jumped me," Gomez said. "Knocked me out cold."

"You sure it was him?" Dean asked.

"Yeah," Gomez replied. He looked apologetically at his commanding officer. "I forgot how big Moore is. I didn't stand a chance."

Dean breathed out hard and shook his head. "He could've killed you right there and then, but he obviously wants to keep you alive."

"He didn't come for me either," Cara pointed out. "Why would Moore immobilize Gomez unless he's got a plan?"

"Oh, I think he does have a plan," Dean replied, pointing to the window. "I think he knocked out Gomez so he could leave us a note."

Cara's eyes followed Dean's finger to the perimeter fence that ran around the cabin. She gasped. There, daubed on the wooden slats in bright red paint, were the words *Psalm 11*.

She flicked through the pages of the Bible as fast as she could.

"Here," she said as her eyes found the correct chapter. She read it out loud. *"Flee, like a bird, to your mountain."*

She looked up at him, remembering the words from the verse the previous day. She repeated them: *"Whenever you hear a word from my mouth, warn them from me."*

"I am the watchman," he said, as the meaning of the message seemed to dawn on him. He turned to her and gripped her hand. *"Flee like a bird.* It's a warning. I don't know how or why, but I have a strong feeling we should leave. Now."

"I'll fetch my rifle," she said, turning to run. She stopped. "Dean," she said, sniffing the air. "What is that smell?"

He flared his nostrils, breathing in the pungent sulfur odor that was pervading the kitchen. He gripped her hand even tighter.

"It's gas," he said. "There's a leak."

"Gas is highly flammable." she said, feeling her breath quicken.

As the reality of their situation took hold, a shot rang out in the distance. It hit the deck and wood splinters flicked up above the windowpane.

He pulled her away from the window and quickly helped Gomez to his feet.

"Let's go," he said, taking her hand and running into the hallway, checking to see that Gomez was right behind.

"I need my rifle," she said, releasing her hand from his and leaving his side. "I must get my rifle."

She bolted into her bedroom and grabbed her rifle bag, hoisting it onto her shoulder. She glanced back to see Dean usher Gomez out the front door and turn to wait for her to return to his side. When she did so, he took her hand once again and raced through the door. Her feet almost left the ground as the force of his grip yanked her into the open air.

She heard another shot ring out.

They made it to the front veranda, still holding hands. The next thing she knew, she was flying through the air, coming to rest with a thud on the muddy ground. Her rifle, and the Bible, landed a moment later.

SIX

Dean pulled himself to his feet, stumbling and coughing amid the black plumes of smoke billowing all around. His ears rang with a high-pitched whine, and he shook his head vigorously, trying to focus on the scene of carnage around him. The cabin had been blown almost entirely apart, and a fierce blaze was taking hold. He spun around, his eyes and ears searching the area for signs of life. His throat burned with an acrid, metallic taste, and he spat on the ground, rubbing the dirt from his face where he had been thrown from the deck. But he was unhurt and had only one thing on his mind.

Then he saw her.

Hanson! God, no.

She was lying on the muddy ground, facedown, her arm outstretched toward her rifle. He ran to her, feeling a sickness rise in his stomach. He'd been in the midst of plenty of explosions during his time in the military but none had given him such a sensation of fear.

He dropped to his knees and carefully checked for broken bones. None. Then he gently rolled her over and checked her pulse. She groaned. A gasp of relief escaped his lips, and he lifted her swiftly into his arms. This was the second time she had been there. It was the second time he had held her limp body in his grasp and prayed for her life.

"I'm fine," she slurred, struggling against the confinement.

"Don't try to move," he said, carrying her through the smoke to the truck. "I've got you."

She weakly pushed his chest with her hands. "My rifle," she said. "Where's my rifle?"

He glanced behind to see her rifle lying on the ground, where it had been blown from her hand.

"I'll fetch it," he said. "Let's get you safe first."

He opened the door of the truck and placed her inside, laying her down across the seat, out of the view from any sniper. He had patched up the battered truck, hammering a wooden board over the broken window. That would give her some protection from the smoke. Or from a bullet. The smokescreen was providing an excellent cloak from gunshots but it wouldn't last too long. He had to leave. Quickly.

He ran back for Cara's rifle, hearing her weakly shout, "And the Bible. Don't leave the Bible."

He snatched the rifle and the Bible from the ground, calling out Gomez's name, desperately hoping to hear a reply.

"Here," came a voice from the smoke. Dean raced to the spot and found Gomez, pinned down by a piece of debris. His face was contorted in pain and frustration.

"I can't move it," he shouted.

Dean summoned all his strength and gripped the piece of heavy wood in his hands. With a huge yell, he lifted the wood just enough for Gomez to slide his leg out. Dean grimaced as he saw the wide red gash on Gomez's thigh. He reached down and hauled the injured man to his feet, helping him hobble to the truck. He'd found his sergeant lying next to the back door of the cabin early that morning, slumped against the wall, looking like he was fast asleep. Dean had instantly regretted leaving his team for the reconnaissance mission. He felt like he'd been duped, especially as the tent had been gone by the time he'd reached the location. Moore had lured him away and taken the opportunity to attack. But he hadn't killed Gomez. And he'd left Hanson alone. Was it only Captain Dean McGovern that Moore truly wanted to hurt? If that were the case, why would Moore warn them about his attack through a Bible verse? Was it even Moore who had written the message? He couldn't be sure of anything. The questions swirling in Dean's head were endless, but he knew that answers would not come easy.

Once Dean had secured both soldiers in the truck, he drove through the scene of desolation and headed for the highway, not sure of where he was going or how he would take care of them. He just needed to get them out of the danger zone and back to safety. Admitting that he was all out of options, he lifted his eyes and silently asked for help.

Cara struggled to sit up, feeling a sense of déjà vu. Dean's arm was around her shoulder, pulling her tightly to him. She felt dizzy but she was thinking clearly. Dean was pushing the truck to its limits, trying to put as much distance between them and the razed cabin in their rearview mirror.

"You okay?" he said, continually glancing at her as she rubbed her head, pulling leaves and mud from her hair.

"Yeah," she said quietly. "You?"

"I'm fine. I got off the easiest. Gomez is hurt pretty bad."

She looked over to Gomez sitting in the seat next to her. He was awake, but his face couldn't contain the pain he felt in his leg. He held the wound tight, clenching his teeth, showing his grit as a Special Forces soldier.

"I'm not hurt badly," he said, snatching at the words. "Don't worry about me. Just get outta here."

"He needs to go to the hospital," Cara said to Dean. "That wound could become infected."

"No!" Gomez shouted. "I'm not going to the hospital. Just get me to a first-aid box and I can take care of this myself." He forced a smile through his pain. "It's just a scratch, no big deal."

Dean leaned over to look at Gomez. "Our first-aid kit is way too basic for your wound, Sergeant," he said. "Hanson's right. You need medical attention."

Gomez banged his head on the headrest. "We should stick together. I don't wanna be the one who bails. I can bear the pain, really."

Cara sat up straight. Gomez's words had jogged her memory, lighting an imaginary bulb over her head. Bear Lake! Why hadn't she thought of it sooner: her family's hunting cabin in Bear Lake, Utah. Her dad was a stickler for safety, always insisting on keeping a large first-aid kit fully stocked in the garage. The cabin was hardly used now. Her mom would visit occasionally, but Cara didn't have the heart to go there anymore. She had no reason to, not till now.

She turned to Dean. "Head for Highway 30. Go west to the border of Utah and Idaho. I know a place."

His arm had never left her side as they'd traveled, his hand firmly planted, fingers splayed on her shoulder. He gave it a squeeze and smiled. "That's the quickest answer to prayer I've ever received."

She smiled back. "Glad I could help."

The cabin was dark as the truck crunched on the leaf-covered driveway. Dean thought it looked a little like a fairy-tale house, nestled in amongst huge, mature, over-hanging trees. But more important, it was secluded, re-mote and secure.

"It's perfect," he said to Cara.

She tried to smile but her expression was apprehen-sive, showing signs of strain. He had moved his arm from her shoulder to concentrate on steering, but her body was still closely pressed against him, and she had been quiet during most of the journey. She'd offered to take a share of the driving but he declined, preferring the reassurance of knowing that she was perfectly shielded in her passen-ger seat by his body. If someone tried to run them off the road, he wanted to be her barrier.

He drove close to the cabin door and switched off the engine, feeling his bones still rattling from the suspen-sion of the rickety, old truck.

"Let's get Gomez inside," he said. "He's our priority for the moment."

She worked with him to lift the sergeant from his seat. Gomez was sleepy, so Dean kept shaking his head, willing him to stay awake until they got him inside and dressed the wound. Cara struggled against the weight of the in-jured man, despite his slight build. Dean noticed her dis-comfort and hoisted Gomez from her grip, heaving him inside and laying him on the large couch in front of the stone-cold hearth.

They worked quickly and efficiently, without the need to speak. Dean laid a fire while Cara fetched the first-aid kit from the garage. As the room warmed up, they cleaned the wound and dressed Gomez's leg, making him as com-fortable as possible. When they'd finished, Cara led Dean into the small kitchen and flicked the switch on the wall.

"We need to eat," she said, rifling through the cup-boards. "Mom always keeps a bunch of nonperishables here." She found some tinned meatballs and dried pasta, holding them up with a smile on her face. "Tonight, we will feast," she said with mock enthusiasm.

He returned her smile but saw that hers didn't extend to her eyes. She didn't seem comfortable here. Although she was usually pretty good at hiding her emotions, he knew her well enough by now to know when she was ill at ease.

"Everything okay, Hanson?" he asked as she busied herself filling a pan with water.

"Sure," she said curtly. He didn't push the matter. Instead, he filled the kettle to make coffee. The long drive had made him lethargic and he wanted to keep his senses alert. He'd been vigilant, but he couldn't guarantee they weren't followed.

Cara filled a glass with water and walked into the living room where Gomez was fast asleep, having been given antibiotics and painkillers. Dean was immensely proud of Cara, remaining so calm and professional, never faltering until Gomez was comfortably settled and his injury treated.

He followed and walked around the room, surveying the rows of trophies, silver cups and rosettes. It was a remarkable record of achievement and he studied each one carefully. The engravings on the trophies seemed to start when she would have been ten years old and stopped abruptly at eighteen.

She stood by the fire, warming her hands. Her clothes were still dirty, from where she'd been thrown from the blast, but she'd washed her face and brushed her hair, revealing a small cut just above her eye. He walked over to her and touched the slight swelling carefully with his forefinger. She winced. He ran his finger along her eyebrow and down the side of her cheek, finally cupping her face with his hand. He did it without thinking, forgetting himself, forgetting that she was his subordinate and he, her commanding officer. He was reminded of this fact when she pulled away and turned her back, staring into the fire.

He put his palm on his forehead. What was he doing? The blast must have affected him more than he realized.

"I'm sorry, Hanson," he said in a low voice. "I'm very proud of you and what you did today. I just wanted to—" he stopped for a moment, searching for the right words "—express my gratitude."

He felt awkward and clumsy, like a teenager again. He was glad that her back was turned so she couldn't see his embarrassment. The last time he'd felt like this was during a disastrous date set up for him by his sister. He hadn't known what to say or do and had blundered through dinner like an idiot. He just didn't know how to behave around women. Should he open doors for them? Offer to pay for dinner? Walk them home? It was a minefield that perplexed him so he preferred to steer well clear. So why were these feelings swirling through his body? Hanson wasn't his date. And never would be.

He took a deep breath and turned to the cabinet on the wall, anxious to change the subject and relieve his tension.

"I've never seen so many trophies in my life," he said. "You clearly had a gift, even when you were a child."

She turned around to face him. Did he see moisture in her eyes?

"I won my first trophy at ten," she said, walking to the cabinet and picking up a discolored silver cup. Her name was embossed on it and she rubbed her finger along the letters, cleaning it up as best she could. "I loved shooting, even when I was a little kid. I loved the feeling of calm, like the world stops before you take a shot. You know when the aim is true—you just know, and the air seems to caress the bullet, carrying it to the center of the target, never deviating or slowing but leaving its mark forever." She smiled. This time, the smile lit up her whole face. "Nothing has ever come close to that. Nothing."

He found himself listening intently to her words, becoming lost in their poetry. He'd never heard anyone talk about a gun that way before. Any man who handled a gun usually considered it a manly tool—something to increase their prowess. To her it was almost spiritual, and it transfixed him.

"I notice the trophies stop when you turned eighteen," he said, walking to a collage of photographs hanging on the wall. He saw a young Cara Hanson beaming widely next to a bearded man wearing a combat vest. They both held Winchester rifles, standing on the porch of the cabin they were occupying at that very moment. "Surely when you're this good, you'd want to carry on competing?" he said, voicing his thoughts aloud.

She put down her glass and went to stand next to him. She pointed to the man in the photograph. "That's my dad," she said flatly. "I stopped competing the day he died." She picked her glass back up and took a gulp of water. "I joined the army instead and the rest is history."

"I'm sorry to hear that, Hanson," he said. "Losing a parent is always hard."

"Did you lose a parent, too?"

He hesitated before answering. "Kind of. My dad is as good as dead to me."

She tilted her head. "That's a shame. I'd give anything to have my dad back. If your dad is still alive, you should treasure the time you have with him."

Dean snorted. "I treasure nothing about my father," he said, feeling old resentments flood to the surface. "He's a coward and bully, and I wish I could erase him from my past."

He looked at Cara to see her staring at him, unblinking. She was clearly shocked at the suddenness of his outburst.

"I envy you, Hanson," he said, lowering his voice again. "Because you had a father who loved you and cherished you and turned you into the extraordinary woman you are today."

He hadn't intended to say those words but he found that they tripped off his tongue on their own. He noticed her swallowing hard as her eyes moistened again, looking as though she would break at any minute.

"And it killed him," she said, a sob finally breaking through the strong facade. "I let him die."

He took a step toward her, reaching out his hand but decided against it.

"How?" he said softly. "What happened?"

She wiped the tears from her cheeks and composed herself. He took her glass from her hand and brought her a tissue from the coffee table. She scrunched it into a ball, twisting it as she spoke.

"We were on a deer hunt not far from here. We'd done hunts like that a thousand times before. I was impatient because Dad couldn't find his combat vest." She looked up at him. "He was such a safety freak, you see. He made me wear a big, bulky, bulletproof vest and I hated it, always complaining about it. I persuaded him to go without it. I said it didn't matter because it was real quiet that winter, and we'd be the only hunters for miles around. Dad used to like trapping, so we went to check on his traps by the lake first. It was such a beautiful day. We talked about practicing for the NCAA Rifle Championships and he said if I worked hard enough, I could even qualify for world-wide competitions." She broke off and breathed deeply.

Dean felt his heart heave for her, for whatever she was about to tell him. He wished he could reach inside and pluck the words out himself, preventing the need for her to say them out loud. But he said nothing. He just listened.

"I didn't want to walk all the way to the lake, so I stayed up high on the hill, waiting for him. Dad was crouching low, adjusting his trap. I saw a deer walk across his path, right in front of him. Dad saw it, too, and he stopped to look at it. It was a lovely moment." She caught her breath. "But then I saw another hunter in the distance. He was tracking the deer. I saw him raise his rifle, and it felt like my stomach dropped out of my body. I tried to shout, but I was too far away, and the wind took my voice in the other direction. I waved my arms, jumped, everything, but Dad was too busy watching the deer. So I loaded my rifle and aimed at the hunter. I was going to shoot his barrel to stop him taking the shot. I knew I could do it. I've hit smaller targets than that a million times before."

She stopped again. He put his hand on her shoulder.

"But you missed," he said gently.

"By a mile," she said, dropping her head. "I wasn't even close."

"And the hunter took his shot?"

"The thing is," she continued, ignoring his question, "my shot spooked the deer and he bolted, leaving Dad totally exposed. It happened in a split second. The hunter took his shot before he realized. I was too late, just a millisecond too late."

Her face had paled, and she hugged herself tightly as she spoke. "If only he'd been wearing his vest."

Dean stood even closer to her, feeling an urgent need to provide some words of comfort and reassurance. "And you blame yourself?"

"Of course I do," she said, knitting her eyebrows together. "It was my fault."

He couldn't stop himself from reaching for her shoulders and drawing her to him. She didn't resist. She rested her head on his shoulder and put her hands on the sides of his waist, as though the fight had left her body. He brought one hand up and placed it on the back of her head, resting his cheek very lightly on her forehead.

"It's not your fault," he whispered. "It's nobody's fault."

She suddenly pushed against him with a power that took him by surprise.

"What would you know?" she challenged. "You weren't there. You have no idea."

Her blue eyes blazed with unexpected ferocity. He knew the anger wasn't directed at him—it was turned inward.

"I know that I'd still rather be in your shoes than mine," he said firmly. "It's far better to lose a loving father than live with a violent one. Don't think of yourself as unlucky, because you're not. You're lucky to have had a beautiful relationship with your dad, no matter what."

She breathed out, as though he'd just winded her.

"I miss him," she said, almost too quietly to hear. "No matter how many shots I make, how many targets I hit, how many lives I save, it's never enough."

"You'll let it go one day," he said, finally understanding why she had an overwhelming need to keep him close and safe. It all made sense now.

"How did you let your dad go?" she asked, looking deeply into his eyes.

"That was easy. I never loved him in the first place."

"That's really sad," she said, furrowing her forehead.

He felt his chest tighten and his heart pick up pace. "I don't think we choose who to love, Hanson. We love those who make us happy, those who are worthy."

"And your dad wasn't worthy?"

"No, he wasn't. But yours was, and that's the only thing you need to remember."

She raised her shoulders and lifted her head, breathing slowly. She opened her mouth to speak, but her attention was caught by an aroma wafting from the kitchen.

"I smell dinner burning," she said, turning quickly and running from the room. He remained standing where he was for a few minutes, reflecting on what had just passed between them. He'd wanted to know, from the first time he'd met her, why a haunted sadness lingered behind her eyes and now he knew. But it didn't help him at all and it certainly wouldn't help their volatile relationship. After witnessing her vulnerability and pain, he knew, without a doubt, that it made him want to protect her even more. And he'd have to fight even harder to suppress it.

Cara stirred the meatballs, chastising herself. Why did she just have to lay her heart open like that? And to her commanding officer, of all people? Now he'd never trust her again—never allow her to fight alongside him as an equal. She shook her head, not quite believing that she'd been so stupid.

"God," she said under her breath, "why did you let him see my weakness?" She looked across the kitchen counter. Dean had brought the Bible in from the truck and placed it next to the kettle. It sat on the counter, prone and silent, inviting her to delve deeper for the true answers. Her faith had been the only thing that kept her going in the months after her dad's death—the one strong pillar to which she clung for dear life.

Dean appeared in the doorway. He saw her eyes resting on the Bible.

"It looks like your theory about the Bible is right, Hanson. Someone does appear to be trying to help us. That message this morning may have saved our lives."

She smiled, wondering how many times scripture had saved her life in the past. She was also pleased that he'd decided to leave their previous conversation in the living room and start over with a new one. He seemed to sense her change of attitude.

"Do you think it's Major Moore?" she asked, trying to return to her professional and efficient manner, hoping to claw back some credibility. "Did you spot anything on your reconnaissance mission to the tent in the hills?"

"The tent had gone by the time I reached the location, but someone had been camping out there watching us, maybe Chris, I don't know." He sighed and shook his head. "If Chris is the man trying to kill me, why would he warn me from danger?"

Cara folded her arms, keeping a distance between them. "Have you ever considered that Moore might not be the enemy you've been told he is?"

"Chris defected over six months ago. There's no way he's on our side."

"Think about it," she said, setting the table for dinner. "Have you ever seen him or even pictures of him with terrorists—anything that would support the theory that he's gone rogue?"

Dean looked at the floor and then back up at Cara. "Come to think of it, no, but that doesn't mean anything. Like I said at the first briefing, his name appears all over secret documents recovered from a raid on a United Free Army sleeper cell three months ago. It's all there in black and white."

She raised her eyebrows. "One thing I've learned from sniper school is never to believe what your eyes can see."

He circled his temples with his forefingers. "Why do you always do this to me?" he asked.

She put down the plates. "Do what?"

"Make me question everything. Make me doubt my own mind."

"All I'm trying to do is help you make up your own mind, not doubt it. Sometimes we don't see what's right in front of us because we think we already know the answers."

He shook his head again. "But I *do* already know the answers," he said as he sat at the table.

Cara dished out their makeshift meal. She sat opposite him, trying to remember the last time she dined alone with a man. It escaped her memory.

"Can I ask you something, Dean?" she said, laying her palms on the table.

"Sure."

"Do you feel the same way about Chris Moore as you do about your father?"

He didn't even need a second to think. "No way."

"Why?"

"Because I've never seen Chris do a bad thing in his life."

She leaned back in her chair and nodded, deciding to leave it at that.

Dean couldn't sleep. His dreams were vivid and strong. A masked man was standing over him with a gun, laughing maniacally. Then the face changed to Cara Hanson's, surrounded by a glow of white light. She lifted him up and held him tight, stilling his beating heart and calming him. But she was in danger! Blood appeared on her torso. He awoke with a start.

He sat up and wiped the sweat from his brow. Cara

was sleeping soundly in the room across the hall. *It's just a dream,* he said to himself, *just a dream.*

He rose from his bed and padded out into the hallway, punching in the intruder alarm code as he walked past the display. Cara told him that her family rarely used the alarm, but she'd remembered how to program it and he'd asked her to set it before they got some rest. He felt much more secure having the reassurance of a warning alert. Otherwise, he probably wouldn't have slept at all. He crept down the stairs to make himself some herbal tea and try to forget the image of the seeping blood stain on Cara's body. *Just a dream,* he reminded himself again.

He checked on Gomez, who was still sleeping soundly on the couch in front of the low-lying fire. He threw on another log. As he walked past the front door, he froze. Someone was turning the handle. The door was bolted tight from the inside so there was no way anyone could enter, even with a key. He stood and listened to the trespasser growing increasingly impatient, finally kicking the door with a firm, angry blow. His instincts took over as his mind still raced with the imagined vision of Cara, bleeding in his arms.

He ran upstairs to fetch his gun, determined that his dream would not turn into reality.

SEVEN

Cara sat bolt upright, her mind switching from slumber to alertness in a split second. She'd heard a creak on the stairs and, listening more intently, she thought she could hear rustling outside. Leaping out of bed, she pulled on her sweatpants and tee, then grabbed her Glock from the nightstand in readiness. Moving quickly to her bedroom door, she opened it a fraction and peered out onto the dimly lit landing. Dean's door was closed, and she assumed he was in a deep sleep inside, unaware of the danger that might have found them already.

Another creak caught her attention. This time, it was on the bare floorboards of the landing. She knew this old cabin like the back of her hand, aware of each groan and creak, able to pinpoint exactly where it was coming from. It would be impossible for anyone to hide from her sight.

The creak was close, right by her door. Summoning all her courage, she threw open her bedroom door and jumped out into the hallway, raising her pistol to shoot. Dean's broad shoulders immediately loomed over her, his gun raised just like hers.

She breathed out and stood down, lowering her weapon to her side. "Dean, you scared the life outta me." She then noticed the look of concern on his face. "What is it? Is someone here?"

He nodded and raised his finger to his lips. He was wearing just jeans and a white, cotton tank top, his dog tags glinting in the soft light. Something had clearly caught him unawares.

"Someone is trying to get in," he whispered. "I heard movement in your room, and I thought you might be in danger. I wanted to check on you before I go investigate."

"I'm coming with you," she whispered back.

She saw the familiar twitch in his cheek, the same twitch that happened each time he wanted to shield her from harm. She didn't wait for him to argue—she simply brushed past him and headed for the stairs, keeping to the sides of the floor where she knew it provided a soundless path. He had no choice but to follow her lead and go to her side. They approached the door together, hearing the intruder scraping at the keyhole, trying to force the lock.

Dean lightly parted the drapes in the living room and squinted out into the darkness. He nodded to Cara and whispered, "Someone is there. You guard Gomez while I deal with this."

Cara cast a glance at Gomez, who remained still and sleeping on the couch. The strong painkillers had totally knocked him out.

"Gomez is fine," she said. "We stand a better chance if we work together. I'll cover your back in case it's a trap. Someone may already be inside."

He looked out the window and back again at her. "Agreed," he said, "but stay real close. I want to feel your back on mine, okay?"

She swiftly moved to his side and stood back-to-back with him. Her head just reached his shoulder blades, and she would be invisible to any assailant behind the door.

They moved in unison to the door and he carefully, and slowly, unbolted it. Her heart thudded as she heard the door handle clunk in his hand.

She felt Dean's back tense when he raised his weapon out in front, throwing the door open wide. She heard a scream: a woman's cry that sounded familiar to her. She spun around and came face-to-face with the last person she expected to see—her mother! And Dean was pointing a gun directly at her chest.

"Mom!" she shouted. She placed her fingers on Dean's hand and pulled his gun downward. "It's okay. It's just my mom."

"Cara!" her mom called, as her hand flew to her mouth. "What on earth is going on? What are you doing here? You never come here."

"Sorry, Mom," Cara said, ushering her inside and closing the door, bolting it behind her. "It's a really long story. We needed a place to go." Her eyes flicked over to Dean. "Work stuff."

"Oh, Cara," her mom said, grabbing her daughter's arm for support. "I thought we were being burglarized. I couldn't find the keys in the flowerpot." She looked Dean up and down, taking in his fierce appearance, still startled by his terrifying introduction. She then noticed Gomez lying on the couch. "Oh, my! How many of you are here?"

"Just the three of us," Cara said reassuringly. "Sergeant Gomez is injured, and we needed a place where we could look after him."

Her mother put a hand to her cheek. "Shouldn't he be in the hospital?"

"We thought it best to look after him ourselves," Cara replied. "It's complicated, but I need to tell you that this is an official military assignment. I'm here as a soldier, not on vacation."

Cara put her arm round her mother and led her into the kitchen to sit. Dean followed and stood in the doorway, while Cara sat opposite her mother and cupped her shaking hands.

She glanced up at Dean. "Could you make some hot tea, please?"

"Sure," he said, "Good idea. I think we could all do with some."

While Dean brewed the tea, Cara noticed her mother eyeing him with wariness. "Mom, this is Dean McGovern," she said. "He's a captain in the U.S. Special Forces and my commanding officer. I'm afraid I can't tell you any more than that, but you can't stay here. It's not safe."

Her mom took a sharp intake of breath. "What do you mean, it's not safe? What's happened?" She gripped Cara's forearm tight. "Are you okay, honey? You're not on the run, are you?"

Cara laughed. "Not exactly, Mom. We're not criminals, if that's what you mean. Like I said, I can't tell you about it. I never expected you to be here. You're supposed to be in Florida."

"I decided to come back from Florida early," she replied. "I should've been here hours ago, but my flight was delayed."

"But why come here instead of home?" Cara asked. "You never told me you were planning a trip to Bear Lake."

"I had a sudden urge to come to the cabin." She looked wistful. "I wanted to be close to him, you know?"

"I know, Mom." Cara held her mother's hands close to her heart. This cabin was where her father's presence weighed heavily in every nook and cranny. It even smelled of him. She both loved and hated it, but she knew she would never let it go.

Dean placed a cup of tea in front of their unexpected guest. "Mrs. Hanson, it's not safe for you to stay here. We need to make arrangements for you to leave immediately. I'll escort you wherever you want to go and make sure you don't get caught up in our current situation."

Cara held up her palm. "Hang on a minute, Dean. She only just got here after a long, delayed flight from Florida, and she's had a big shock. She doesn't need to leave right away."

Dean stared past Cara to the elegant, silvery-blond-haired lady seated at the table. "Try not to worry, Mrs. Hanson. I'll take care of everything for you."

"Please," she said, relaxing her guard, "call me Sheila."

He smiled and said, "I'll leave you two to talk, and we can make plans to get you on your way, Sheila."

As he left the kitchen, Cara got up and followed him into the living room. She tugged his arm at the foot of the stairs and stood before him with her arms crossed, trying hard to retain her composure.

"Just who do you think you are? You totally ignored me in there and rode roughshod over everything I said."

He ran his fingers through his curly black hair. "It's not safe for her here, you know that. She should leave right away."

"I agree," said Cara, clenching her fists, "but it's the middle of the night. She's tired and scared. She should get some rest before we take her home."

"May I remind you, Hanson," he said, returning to the stern persona she'd met on that sunny day in the Colorado hills, "that I am in command of this mission. This is my call."

She pulled herself up to her full height. "You may be in command of this mission, sir, but you are not in command of my mother."

His face hardened and he clenched his jaw tightly, yet she continued to bore her eyes into his, sensing that the fire of antagonism between them had once again started to catch. But there was no way she was going to back down. Not on this subject.

Dean looked from Cara to the doorway of the kitchen where Sheila Hanson was still sitting, visibly trembling as she brought the tea to her lips. His eyes narrowed, watching the shaken woman place a palm to her forehead and lean heavily on her elbow. A breath caught in his chest and he glanced at the gun in his right hand before looking back up into Cara's face.

"She'll need to be constantly guarded," he said.

Cara uncrossed her arms and nodded her head. "I'll make up a bed for her and we can take turns keeping watch. She'll leave first thing in the morning."

"I'll take her wherever she needs to go," he said quickly.

Cara tilted her head to one side. "I think we should wait until we know what my mom wants first. Let's ask her before we make any definite plans."

He breathed hard, cracking the fingers of his left hand. She knew she was riling him, pushing all the buttons that sent sparks through the air. But she didn't care. After the weakness she'd displayed the previous day, she was determined to redeem herself and to prove that she was a strong and capable soldier, able to take charge and lead with authority. And, she reminded herself, this was *her* mom, not his. She knew what was best in this situation and she strongly felt that Dean's judgment was impaired, clouded by events he kept close to his heart. This was *her* call.

He turned and began to walk up the stairs. "I'm going to get a sweatshirt. I'll take the first watch."

"Fine," she said, watching him stride up the stairs two at a time.

She pursed her lips and blew out her cheeks. This man was totally infuriating. He brought out the best and worst in her, and she was powerless to control it. She felt like she'd started walking down a path that had taken on a life of its own. She longed for all this to be over so she could return to normal life—a life without the emotional roller coaster that Dean seemed to be leading her on. Once she'd neutralized the threat he was facing, she intended to hotfoot it from his life forever, no matter how difficult it would be. In this situation, she must allow her head to overrule her heart.

Dean muttered to himself as he dressed, roughly pulling on a long-sleeved shirt and sweatshirt, shaking his head.

"Calm down, Dean, just take it easy," he said to himself through gritted teeth.

He was used to being the one who gave orders, not the one taking them, especially from a junior rank. Her insubordination now meant that he had two women to protect instead of one, as well as an injured man. He sat on the edge of the bed to compose himself and breathe deeply, remembering that a cool head was his strongest weapon in dangerous circumstances.

Sheila Hanson was a mirror image of Cara—just a couple of decades older—with the same waiflike figure. He wondered if her interior was as stubborn and determined as her daughter's. Seeing her sitting at the kitchen table, shaken and afraid, had tugged deeply on his heartstrings, unleashing memories that he usually kept on a tight rein. He knew that Sheila Hanson wasn't Diane McGovern; his mom didn't even resemble Cara's. But she still needed looking after, protecting and removing from the menace that was ever present around them. Sheila Hanson's unannounced arrival had transported him back to those times when he would drive his mom to his grandmother's house, two blocks away, before returning home to deal with his father's rage. His first, and only, thought was to get her away from danger and deliver her to safety. That instinct ran so deep in his psyche that it seeped into his bones. And no matter how hard he tried, it defined him as a man and always would—he was a protector to the core. The trouble was, so was Cara.

He checked his pistol and ensured it was fully loaded. He counted his bullets, hoping it would be enough for the duration. He didn't know how long they would remain at the cabin but he knew that Gomez wasn't well enough to travel, and his priority at that moment was to get Sheila Hanson far away from this place before making any more decisions—decisions that could mean the difference between life and death.

Cara's words over dinner had given him food for thought. He had always assumed that the evidence he'd seen regarding Chris's defection was enough to prove his guilt. He'd never stopped to really consider it, to think of the man he knew Chris to be, the man who would lay down his life to save others. Could he ever dare hope that Chris remained that same man, that the evidence was wrong? One thing was certain: *someone* was trying to help them, using the power of scripture to convey warnings that had kept them safe thus far.

He stood up, reluctantly admitting that Cara's lightness of touch had made him reassess his mission. He couldn't be sure any longer that Chris Moore was the true enemy, and he would need to keep his wits about him to figure out the truth—his wits and, of course, Cara Hanson, who planted seeds of ideas in his head that he watered in times of reflection. He bent his head and allowed the anger to flow from his body. He'd often been accused of being too headstrong, refusing to bend to others' points of view, especially since he'd left the church. Maybe they were right, maybe Cara was right.

He raised his eyes and nodded his head. "Yeah, I know," he said to the air, "she's like the other half of me. I'm not perfect, either."

He holstered his gun and walked down the stairs, feeling a renewed sense of calm wash over him. How did she do this to him? She drove him to the brink and then pulled him back again when he contemplated her reason and logic. She, and only she, had ever made him think so deeply about things he'd always accepted were true.

He checked on Gomez and walked into the kitchen. Cara was sitting at the table with her mom, deep in conversation. They both looked up as he entered the room, and their faces took on expressions that he couldn't fathom. Cara's eyes ran over his body from head to toe, and she gave a small gasp, reaching for her mom's hand.

He looked down at himself, momentarily confused, before it dawned on him—he was wearing Cara's dad's clothes! She'd given them to him while his own mud-covered pants and sweatshirt were being washed.

Sheila smiled, bringing her hand to her cheek. "My husband was a tall man, like you. You look just like him wearing that sweatshirt." She turned and whispered to Cara. "It's nice to have a man around the place again."

"He's not staying here forever, Mom," said Cara. She looked at Dean with steely eyes. "He's just visiting."

Dean leaned against the doorframe and said nothing, having decided that things seemed to work a lot better when he kept his mouth shut.

"Mom and I have decided to go to the town of Hurricane tomorrow," Cara said, rising to wash the glasses in the sink. "It's in South Utah, about three hundred and fifty miles away. My aunt lives there and Mom will stay with her for a few days before going home. It's the safest option. I can be there and back in a day."

Dean chewed on his lip, calculating the distance and time for the journey. "*You* can be there and back in a day."

Cara dried her hands on a dishcloth. "We'll leave at nine a.m. Mom drove a rental car here from the airport so I'll use that. She said she'd extend the terms, and we can keep it for as long as we need it. I don't think I could stand another long journey in that shaky old truck."

"So it's all decided, then?" Dean asked, biting his tongue to stop the argumentative words fighting their way from his mouth.

"It's all decided," she said curtly. "You don't need to worry about a thing."

He looked at the ceiling. "Believe me—I've got a whole lot to worry about."

Cara and her mom laid sheets on the small bed in the guest room upstairs. It had always been her room as a child during the summer months, when the beautiful turquoise waters of Bear Lake became their second home.

"You okay, honey?" asked her mom. "You seem a little tense."

"I'm fine," she answered. "It's just hard being back here, you know?"

Sheila Hanson smoothed the white cotton sheets along the edge of the mattress. Cara caught sight of the thin gold band she still wore on the third finger of her left hand. Sheila sat on the bed, looking up into her daughter's face.

"Your dad would be pleased to see you using the place again," she said. "A cabin like this needs to have air breathed into it and hear laughter in its walls." She looked down into her hands. "The sounds of a family."

Cara sat beside her. "*We* are a family, Mom, you and me."

Her mom laughed. It was a high, brittle laugh that sounded like breaking glass.

"I'm talking about your own family, Cara. You deserve the same happiness that I had when I was your age."

Cara took a deep breath. "I *am* happy, Mom."

She slumped forward. Who was she kidding? She couldn't fool her mom any more than she could fool herself. She could pinpoint the exact moment when happiness whooshed from her body, to be replaced with a willful determination that had swallowed her whole life. Being happy again was not an option, not while people needed her protection.

Sheila took Cara's hand in hers. She held it tight. "You know your dad would never have blamed you for what happened. Nobody blamed you."

"*I* blame me," Cara said, rising to stand by the window. "If I'd managed to keep my composure, I'd have prevented the accident from happening and Dad would still be here with us. It's my fault he wasn't wearing a vest." She shook her head. "Every shot I've made since that time brings me a little step closer to making amends."

Her mom sighed. "Does it, Cara? Does it, really?"

She didn't answer the question and lightly parted the drapes to stare out into the blackness of night. Dean was walking around the small silver sedan that her mom had driven from the airport, checking it over, making sure it was ready for their journey in the morning. He seemed to sense her eyes upon him and looked up, catching her gaze, holding it firm. His expression was sad, with a resignation she hoped didn't mean he had given up the fight. He pulled the collar of her dad's shirt around his neck and turned back to the car, popping the hood, obscuring himself from view. She felt a reluctant sense of reassurance, knowing he was backing her up, ready to catch her when she fell. And she'd fallen twice already—from the anaphylaxis and the explosion at the cabin in Wyoming. He'd been there to pick her up, keep her safe and get her strong again. When she'd allowed him to take her into his arms, just for the briefest of moments, she'd glimpsed how it would feel to let go. And it had both comforted and terrified her all at the same time. She had exposed her vulnerability almost entirely, and as a woman in a man's world, she knew that displaying such sentiment would undermine her status as a soldier. One of her colleagues had once told her, "Real soldiers don't cry," and she'd resolved to bury her emotions deep, in case she marked herself out as the weakest link.

"Honey, you need to get some sleep." Her mom's words brought her back into the room. "We've got a long drive tomorrow."

She saw Dean close the hood and wipe his hands on an oily rag.

"You're right," she said, turning away from the window. "Dean or I will be right outside your room all through the night." She smiled. "Don't worry about a thing, Mom."

Sheila Hanson pushed herself up from the bed and wrapped her arms around her daughter. "I'm not worried, honey. You two are the best bodyguards anyone could ask for."

In the morning, Dean sat down at the kitchen table opposite Cara with a heavy heart. He'd try one last time.

"Hanson," he said, waiting for her to look up before continuing. "The car is ready to go. There's a first-aid box, flares and blankets in the trunk."

He took a deep breath, but she raised her hand to cut him off. "I'm still going," she said, "and I won't discuss it any further."

He closed his mouth. She'd shored up her defenses good and tight this time. He decided to take a leaf out of Cara's book and use a lighter touch.

"I like your mom," he said, smiling. "She's a kind-hearted lady." He looked behind Cara's shoulder to where Sheila Hanson was fussing around a bemused Sergeant Gomez, adjusting his blankets and plumping his pillows.

Cara glanced behind. "Yeah," she laughed, "that's my mom all right."

"Does she come here often?"

Cara leaned back, regarding him suspiciously. "A few times a year. She keeps it nice and stops it from looking neglected."

"She does a good job," he said, looking around at the matching gingham curtains and cushions. "It's real homey."

"Yeah," she said, seeming to appreciate these small touches that had escaped her notice. "It does look nice."

"Thank you for bringing us here," he said. "I appreciate how hard it was to come back to this cabin, but you did it for me—me and Gomez."

"I'd do whatever it takes to keep you safe, Dean."

He smiled. "And you're doing a great job. I don't think I've told you that before."

She seemed to be stunned into silence for a few seconds before asking, "Are you complimenting me?"

He threw back his head and laughed. Had he really been so hard on her that words of praise took her by such surprise?

"I'm sorry, Hanson," he said quietly, leaning toward her across the table. "It's been hard for me to stand back and let you do your job. I know I'm difficult to live with, pigheaded and stubborn, but I want to try and change."

She narrowed her eyes and leaned forward to meet his posture. Her cross fell from her shirt and dangled from its chain, an inch above the table. "We all want to change," she said. "But it's not that easy. It takes a lot of hard work."

His eyes came to rest on the swinging rhythm of the silver cross.

"I think I may know someone who can help me," he said with a wink.

She nodded slowly. "Well, it's a good start." She checked her watch and drained her cup, before standing and putting her hand on her holstered gun.

"It's time for me to leave," she said.

He stood to face her. "You look tired. You didn't sleep much last night." He puffed out his chest. "I feel good, refreshed. Maybe I should do the long drive today while you get some rest."

She walked over to him, to stand just inches away and smiled directly into his face.

"Nice try, Dean."

He shook his head and grinned. "It was worth a try, huh?"

They remained standing inches apart as Sheila Hanson entered the kitchen and busied herself washing dishes.

Cara stepped back and looked over to her mother. "It's time to leave, Mom. You ready?"

"Yes, honey. I'll just finish these dishes and fetch my bag." She looked out of the window into the small meadow beyond the low picket fence. "Oh," she said with nervous surprise in her voice. "It looks like someone left a note of some kind."

Cara leaped forward. "What are you talking about, Mom?"

Her mother pointed to a tree a hundred yards in the distance. On the rough brown bark was a white piece of paper, fluttering in the breeze, pinned to the trunk with a small knife.

Cara's eyes flew to Dean's. He was already on the case, having pulled Mrs. Hanson away from the window and drawn his gun.

EIGHT

Cara grabbed Dean by his arm. "Let me scope out our surroundings first," she said. "Don't go out there until we know it's safe."

"Okay," he said. "I'll guard your mom while you work."

She ran upstairs to fetch her binoculars and her rifle, then worked her way around each window, thoroughly checking the terrain for signs of danger. Trusting in her finely honed instincts, she satisfied herself that no one was lying in wait, and they could retrieve whatever message had been left for them to find.

She ran back downstairs into the kitchen. "It's safe," she said breathlessly. "I'll go get it."

"No," he said, pressing her shoulders. "I'll get it. Wait here."

Before she could object, he darted out the door and was flitting through the long grass to snatch the message from the tree. He returned holding the paper in one hand and a small, intricately carved knife in the other.

"It's Chris Moore's knife," he said. "I'd know it anywhere."

"What's written on the paper?" she asked.

"You read it," he said, handing it to her. She saw his eyes flick to the Bible on the counter and she knew, in an instant, that it was another verse.

She looked at the familiar black, scrawled writing. *"John 14:1."*

She turned to her mother. "Mom, can you go sit with Sergeant Gomez while I talk to Dean?"

As soon as her mother was out of sight, Cara grabbed the Bible from the kitchen counter and riffled through its pages, coming to a stop on the chapter of Saint John. She read the words, *"Do not let your hearts be troubled. Trust in God; Trust also in me."*

Dean let his head drop, searching the floor for answers. Cara put the open book on the table, letting the words remain visible in the silence.

"He's asking us to trust him," she said, finally. "Why?"

"He's planning something." Dean glanced warily through the kitchen window. "He's preparing the groundwork, telling us to follow his lead."

"Should we trust him?"

Dean stood in front of her and gripped her by the shoulders. "We trust nothing and no one."

She stared at him. "Not even scripture?"

She saw his breathing quicken. "I want to believe it, I really do, but I can't let Chris fool me again."

"You're not even sure that he fooled you once. You said yourself that you've never seen him do a bad thing in his life. You want to trust him, and you want to trust in the scripture he's showing us."

"What if you're wrong? What if he's out there, waiting to draw us in, ready to attack?"

She saw his upper body rise and fall even faster. This time, she *did* put a palm on his chest to calm him. It worked; he stilled. "He saved us in Wyoming, didn't he?"

Dean drew a deep breath. "Maybe he saved us from the explosion because he's planned a fate far worse than a quick death?" He looked into her face, revealing a rare glimpse of fear beneath his tough exterior. "Maybe he wants hostages rather than bodies."

Cara looked down at the Bible on the table. Try as she might, she couldn't bring herself to accept that God would allow His Word to be used in that way.

"I want to trust Major Moore," she said. "We should keep an open mind. I can't be sure that the mission objective is still valid, so I won't shoot to kill him any longer. If I get a chance to take him out, I'll shoot to wound."

"Whatever happens," he said, touching her hand on his chest, "you need to keep yourself safe. Forget about me. Just keep yourself safe."

She could feel his heart beating beneath his shirt and heard the seriousness, the passion, in his voice. She pulled her hand away.

"Are you kidding?" she said. "This is all the more reason for me to keep you close. If Moore has found us, and we don't know what he intends to do, then you need me more than ever."

He sighed and ran his fingers through his hair. "If you lose your weapon or you run out of ammo, you're totally exposed."

"I won't lose my weapon," she said, resting her hand on top of her gun. "Trust me, Dean, I can do this."

He let his hand drop to his side. "Why don't we all go to Hurricane together?" he said. "It's safer that way."

"No," she protested. "We can't move Gomez yet. We don't even know the extent of the damage to his leg. Someone needs to stay here to protect him."

He looked to the ceiling and brought his hands to his face, palms together, like a gesture of frustrated prayer.

"Then let me go to Hurricane. You stay here with the doors bolted."

"No," she said again. "It's all been decided." She folded

her arms. "I thought you said you wanted to change, but you're still trying to shield me from danger. You have no faith in me at all."

He sighed and ran a hand over his face. "Someone followed us here. Or maybe they followed your mother. I don't know how it keeps happening, but Moore keeps finding us, and if you go out alone, there's a good chance you'll be followed again."

She crossed her arms. "I'll handle it."

He thought for a moment. "Is there a cell phone in the cabin?"

"Yeah, it's pretty old but it works."

"Take it with you," he said. "I'll activate my cell phone so you can check in with me every hour." He bent down to look her in the eye. "And I mean every hour. I want to know where you are at all times, okay?"

"But won't that expose us to tracking?" she asked.

"It's too late to worry about that, Hanson. If you're in danger, at least I'll know where to start looking for you."

"But you can't leave Gomez, not even for me."

He shook his head. "That's my offer, Sergeant. Take it or leave it. Don't make me pull rank on you."

She stared at him. "I'll take the cell phone, but only if you promise not to leave Sergeant Gomez to come to my rescue."

He blinked slowly. "I can't make that promise. Gomez may be injured, but he's still a Special Forces soldier, trained to survive."

"Then it's no deal," she said defiantly.

"I don't want to fight with you again," he said, his face taking on a pained expression. "I meant it when I said I wanted to change. I know you're strong and able to look after yourself, but this is a whole new ball game for me."

He held up his hands. "I'm trying really hard here, Hanson."

A smile crept across her face in spite of the potential new level of danger. Finally, they seemed to be making progress.

"Why don't we compromise?" she said, glancing over her shoulder to where her mother was deep in conversation with Gomez. "If you feel the need to come to my aid, you take Sergeant Gomez to the nearest hospital first."

He nodded. "Agreed." He put his hand on her shoulder. "You drive me mad, you know that?"

"I know I may seem stubborn to you, but I need to get my mom to safety," she said. "I need to see with my own eyes that she's out of harm's way. I know that may be hard for you to understand but it's how I feel."

He sat down on a chair and leaned on his knees. "It's not hard for me to understand at all," he said quietly. "I totally understand."

In that moment he looked more fragile to her. She saw the lines and creases around his mouth for the first time. She saw the way a curl of hair had strayed onto his forehead. She saw black eyelashes framing eyes that kept up a constant guard. She saw his face in its individual parts, realizing that she'd never really *seen* him before, not like this.

"Your mom?" she asked.

He nodded. "I took my mom to safety more times than I care to remember," he said, not looking at her. "Having your mom here brought back old memories. I'm sorry if I overreacted."

"It's okay," she said, remembering his brutal description of his father and reading between the lines.

He said nothing.

"Is your mom safe now?" she asked tentatively. "From your dad, I mean."

He looked up. "Yeah, she's safe now. My dad's serving two life sentences in jail."

"I'm sorry, Dean."

He gave a hollow laugh. "Don't feel sorry for me, Hanson. Feel sorry for the two people he shot and killed in a bar in New Mexico." He looked up into her face, and she saw the unadulterated pain in his eyes. "He got into a fight. He killed two men because they knocked over his beer." He shook his head. "I'll never understand it."

She closed her eyes, remembering Dean's words about her being blessed to have a father like hers. Suddenly, she really did feel like the luckiest person in the world. Her dad had left her with a precious legacy that had been denied to Dean. He would live forever in the knowledge of what his father was, and he would carry the scars in his heart forever.

She walked to his chair and put a hand on his head—his hair felt wiry like wool. She hoped she wasn't overstepping the mark, but it felt right. He moved his head slightly against her touch and said, "What's happening here, Hanson?"

"I don't know," she whispered. "I guess we just have to wait and see what happens."

He reached up and seized her hand, pulling it close to his cheek. He raised his head to look into her eyes and said, "I wasn't talking about Moore."

She blinked under his powerful gaze. "I know."

Sheila Hanson called out that it was time to go, and the moment was broken.

Cara turned to leave the kitchen, but Dean grabbed her arm and pulled her back, bringing his mouth close to her ear. "Let's put this on hold for now, okay?"

She nodded, feeling the need to leave the stifling atmosphere of the cabin, and run out into the fresh air outside. She almost fled from the room.

Dean watched the small silver sedan drive away into the distance, sending reddish-brown leaves swirling in its path. He wanted to run after the car and demand that Cara yield to his authority. He'd wanted to issue an order than she remain within his sight at all times, but he knew it was pointless. Once Cara Hanson made up her mind, nothing could change it. If she wanted to place herself on the front line of danger, who was he to stop her? It was a battle he thought he could win, but it turned out to be a war he'd well and truly lost.

He followed the car to the end of the driveway, watching it fade to a dot in the distance, making sure that no one was tailing her. He dropped his shoulders and headed inside, intending to spend the day looking after Gomez and waiting by the phone for her calls. Once she returned, he would ask her to return to base with Gomez. The injured sergeant would be well enough to travel in a day or two. Dean felt his control of their situation slipping from his grasp, and he and Cara were always at risk of clashing again. He knew she needed to see her mother to safety, but after that he intended to take charge again—if only in a professional sense.

He closed his eyes and bolstered his belief that Cara would return to her Bobcats regiment unscathed. She would leave his team, allowing his life to go back to how it always used to be—controlled, disciplined and uncomplicated. It was a routine he'd almost forgotten in these few, short days. He marveled at how easily his life had unraveled, creating a feeling of helplessness that he'd never known before. He sat on the porch step, remembering the very first time he'd seen her face, mostly obscured by camouflage and paint. But he'd known she was special, even then. He stood and kicked the wooden step, angry with himself for not listening to his instincts when he'd wanted to block her entry into his team. He should've known better, and now he was in deep. The connection between them had gone beyond that of commander and subordinate, and he had strayed into territory that was even more dangerous than the terrorists. And he had no weapons to fight a war of the heart.

"So, tell me more about the captain." Sheila Hanson's voice was light and teasing. "You two seem to be close."

Cara shook her head. "He's my commanding officer, Mom, that's all."

"That's all, huh?"

"Yes."

"Oh, honey, I see the way he looks at you. Trust me, I know that look."

"What look?"

"*That* look. I remember seeing it when I met your dad."

Cara straightened up in her seat. "He doesn't look at me like that, Mom. We fight all the time. He's stubborn and difficult, and he drives me totally mad."

Her mom laughed. "I'm sure I don't know anyone else who's stubborn and difficult."

"Okay. Point taken. But we're completely incompatible. He's not interested in a strong woman like me." Despite his good intentions, she knew they were a match made in a fireworks factory, just waiting for someone to light the touch paper.

"He's a good man, Cara, I can see it."

She nodded in agreement. "I know that. I see his integrity and moral values, but he's so old-fashioned in his views." She thought of how hard she'd had to push to fight alongside him. Yet she still felt she had a long way to go. "I'd never fit in with his idea of the perfect woman."

"No woman is the perfect woman, Cara. She can only ever be the right woman."

Cara sighed. "And I'm *not* the right woman for him."

Her mom settled back into her seat, leaning her head against the headrest to watch the countryside pass them by.

"I don't want you to spend your life alone, honey. You're twenty-five now and all you do is work. It's time to let go of the past and move on with your life."

Cara gripped the wheel tight. "Not this again, Mom. I'm okay as I am. I don't need a man in my life."

Her mom looked over at her and lightly touched her forearm. "Sometimes, we don't realize how hard it is to be strong all the time, not until we meet someone who wants to share the burden."

Cara's breath caught in her throat. "I *am* strong. I can't afford to be weak in my job. It undermines everything I do."

"Being weak isn't a weakness, Cara. Try to remember that. Everyone needs help sometimes, even you."

Cara kept her eyes firmly focused on the road ahead, trying not to let her mom's words invade her too deeply. She'd felt cracks starting to appear in her defenses ever since starting this mission, and she was trying hard to paper over them.

"I'm fine, Mom," she reiterated. "Try not to worry about me."

Sheila Hanson breathed out heavily. "I hope you get to experience the kind of love I felt with your dad." She made a soft murmuring sound. "Seeing the captain dressed in your dad's shirt took me back to the old days. He reminds me so much of your father."

"He's nothing like Dad," said Cara, shaking her head.

Her mom smiled. "Oh, he sure is, honey. I just think that you don't want to see it."

Cara decided to say no more. She didn't want to talk about her dad or Dean. She didn't want to talk at all, and the rest of the journey passed in a blur of her mom's chit-chat as she told Cara about redecorating the house and planting in the garden. She was grateful for the subject matter; it was safe, unchallenging. Every hour, as prom-ised, she called Dean, noticing that the phone was an-swered immediately. He couldn't mask the anxiety in his voice.

Finally at her destination, Cara left her mom in a flurry of kisses and hugs, relieved that she was safe and sound, far away from the danger-filled life that awaited Cara upon her return. She began the journey back just as dusk was falling, and tiredness took hold of her. She pressed the ac-celerator and kept on going, using her military training to overcome fatigue with mind exercises. She was so tired that she almost missed the high-beam car headlight in her rearview mirror—almost! It was a large black SUV with one headlight smashed and broken—the headlight she'd taken out with her rifle.

The tiredness melted from her body like ice, leaving her with a sharpness of mind that took her to autopilot. She swerved across the quiet road, realizing that her small economy sedan was no match for the power of the SUV. She lifted her eyes. *I could do with some help here,* she pleaded. Dean's words instantly returned to her: *In a game of cat and mouse, the only safe option is to be the cat.* With that in mind, she turned sharply onto a dirt road, leading to a nature park. It would be quiet and secluded with no danger of civilians being hurt.

The SUV was almost upon her, nudging her bumper

and sending her car skipping forward. She flipped the popper on her holster and placed her hand on the handle of her gun. Her rifle would be useless in this situation. Dean had been right—a handgun was the only way to protect herself in close combat, and she was glad he'd had the presence of mind to plan ahead for her. The tires crunched on the wood chip of a leafy parkland, providing the perfect place to stop. She yanked the wheel quickly and brought her foot down heavily on the brake, sending the car skidding into a 180-degree turn. The driver of the SUV was taken by surprise and slammed into her hood, deploying her airbag and shrouding her view. They were facing each other, hood to hood, as the dust settled and an eerie calm descended. But she knew she had the upper hand. She had been prepared.

Punching her seat belt, she jumped from the car and discharged her weapon, using the car door for protection. She was conscious of the need to keep momentum on her side and darted from behind her car door to the door of the SUV. A man was inside, his head flopped onto the airbag on the steering wheel. He was wearing a ski mask, but she could tell he was dazed by the impact. She took her chance. Opening the door, she grabbed his black sweater and used all her strength to jerk him from the car. He fell easily, landing with a heavy thud on the dusty ground. The passenger seat was empty, so she hopped onto the step, ready to slide into the driver's seat of the SUV, its engine still running and its bodywork in a lot better shape than her own small sedan. Then she felt fingers close around her ankle and a force pulled her back. She raised her other leg and kicked down hard, making contact with a rigid surface beneath. There was a crack and a howl, indicating that a bone had been broken. It was obviously painful enough for the man to release his grip and allow her to scramble into the driver's seat while pushing the airbag through the steering wheel to enable her to drive without constraint.

She put the stick in reverse and floored the accelerator, making another 180-degree turn. As she made her escape, the man lay writhing on the ground in the dust. But he staggered to his feet, holding his left arm close to his side and raising the right one to shoot. He ran after the vehicle, shooting as he did so. She swerved from side to side, keeping him in her sights at all times, narrowing her eyes at the flicker of recognition he'd awakened in her. Something in his gait made her look twice, certain that she'd seen it before.

She tried to concentrate on the road ahead, hoping there were no police-patrol cars in the area. With one headlight out and a crumpled hood, the battered SUV was a prime target to be pulled over. She checked her rearview mirror constantly, determined not to be followed again. She knew that the man in the ski mask was not Moore—he was way too small to be the tall major, but she felt a malevolence flowing from him that made her arm hairs stand on end. She could sense he was consumed by bitterness and spite. She reached for the cell phone to call Dean and sighed heavily, realizing that she had left it on the passenger seat of the sedan. She knew he would quickly worry without her calls.

After four hours of anxiously driving along winding country roads, her spirit lifted to see the cabin come into view. It was fortunate the roads had been quiet, and she'd been able to slip through them unnoticed. She turned slowly onto the tree-lined driveway and her headlight illuminated a figure sitting on the porch step. It was Dean. He saw the SUV and sprang into action, jumping up, raising his gun and running toward the car.

"Out of the car," he shouted. "Hands in the air."

"It's okay, it's okay," she called, jumping out of the vehicle. "It's me."

He raced to her and ran his eyes all over her body,
checking for injuries. "Are you hurt?" he asked, taking
her head in his hands to study her eyes. "Any concussion,
dizziness, blurred vision?"

She took his hands from her head. "I'm fine. I ran into
a bit of trouble but I took care of it."

He looked relieved. "What happened?" he asked. "You
stopped calling. Is your mom safe?"

"Mom is safe," she confirmed, "but someone tried to
run me off the road, and I lost the cell phone." She rubbed
her eyes.

"You look exhausted, Hanson," he said, putting his arm
around her shoulder and leading her to the passenger door.
She slid inside and leaned back in the seat as Dean drove
the car to the door of the cabin.

"Are you sure you're not hurt?" he asked, unable to
hide the concern on his face.

"I told you already. I took care of it. There's not a
scratch on me. Let's get inside and I'll debrief you."

"Okay, Sergeant," he said, assuming a more professional military style.

They exited the vehicle and inspected the damage to
the hood.

"Just bodywork," Dean said. "I can fix this." He
checked the glove compartment for paperwork—none.
"We'll need to ask someone trustworthy to run a check
on the plates. It may lead us right to the top of the UFA."

Gripped by weariness, lightheadedness overcame her,
and she leaned against the side of the car, feeling herself
slide on the smooth metal. Dean propped her up with his
strong arms.

"You need to rest, Hanson. Let's get you inside."

She leaned against his firm grip and walked up the step, onto the porch, before something caught her eye in the distance. She squinted into the darkness.

"No, no, no," she said, panicking. "I let someone follow me. How could I have been so stupid?"

She pointed to the quiet road that led to their driveway. About a quarter mile away, parked up on the side of the road was the battered and bruised silver sedan, headlights dimmed but still running.

"I didn't think it was still drivable," she gasped. "I'm so sorry, Dean. I led them right to you. It's not Moore; it's someone else."

"We knew it was only a matter of time before others turned up," Dean said, opening the front door and ushering her inside. "The important thing is that you're back safe."

"But I've put you in danger." She shook her head.

"I can handle it," he said, pulling her through the door and bolting it behind her. "It's not your job to worry about me."

She watched him work his way around the windows and doors, securing their location. She muttered under her breath, chastising herself harshly. This was her fault. She had messed up and led the enemy to the gates. Exhaustion or not, it would now be her job to guard those gates and stop the enemy from breaking through.

NINE

Dean darted through the cabin, thankful that Cara had managed to fend off an attack and return to him without injury. She recounted the experience as he worked his way around all possible entrances for an intruder, shuddering as she reached the part when her attacker had tried to drag her back from the SUV. She'd had a close escape. He wished he could've prevented it and taken her place instead. But she would never allow that to happen.

When she'd finished, she rubbed her face, dropping her eyelids with the tiredness that was close to overwhelming her. "I'm so sorry, Dean," she repeated. "I was careless in being followed."

She balled her hands into fists. "I was tired. I should've immobilized the sedan before coming here. I can't believe I messed up like that."

"You didn't mess up, Hanson," Dean said, placing his hands on her shoulders and bending to meet her eyes. You got your mom to safety. That was your objective for today."

"Yeah," Gomez called from the sofa, "and it sounds like you managed to break the arm of one of the terrorists. I'd say that was a pretty good day."

Dean slapped his hand to his head. Gomez! In the suddenness of the drama, he'd forgotten about the injured man on the sofa.

"Gomez," he said. "We need to move you to a more secure room until we know what level of threat is out there." He turned to Cara. "Help me get him upstairs. We can put him in the safest room at the back."

Cara helped Dean walk Gomez up the stairs although, like last time, he took the bulk of the weight. He didn't need her help to move the sergeant—he just wanted to keep her in his sight. They settled him in a room, armed him with a gun and locked him inside. They then stood together on the landing outside his room for a few seconds, saying nothing, mentally preparing for the storm ahead.

"I need to get my rifle," she said, "and set up a lookout post."

"Hanson," he said quietly. "You're in no shape to pick up a weapon. You're tired and weak. You need to sleep."

He saw her face flinch and fall but she didn't argue. Not yet, anyway. He decided to continue.

"Let me assess whatever is out there while you rest. I'll make sure no one gets in. Nothing will happen, I promise."

Her eyes seemed to lose focus and look right through him. "Being weak isn't a weakness," she murmured, not to him but to herself.

"I'll take the strain for you," he whispered. "Just let it go for now."

He could almost hear the thoughts that were spinning through her head. He knew how she struggled to relinquish control, how she desperately wanted to make amends for the past and right the wrong that had happened here seven years ago. The trouble was, as she admitted herself, nothing she could do was ever enough. He felt the connection between them grow stronger than ever, desperately hoping that she would take this tiny step toward healing by shifting just a small portion of her burden onto him.

She nodded. "Okay," she said. "I can't even think straight let alone shoot straight." She looked up and smiled feebly. "I haven't missed a shot in seven years. I don't want to start now."

She turned and walked slowly to her bedroom door, casting a backward glance at him, looking up and down at the jeans and shirt he wore—things of her father's that hadn't been worn in over seven years.

"Those clothes suit you, you know?" she said, opening the door. "You can keep them if you like."

"Thanks," he said. "I will."

As soon as he heard the lock of her door click in place, he sprang into action. He turned off every light in the cabin and set up a lookout post in an upstairs window. The sedan was still there, sitting in the road but the lights were off and, using his binoculars, he could see that no one was inside. He searched the foliage surrounding the cabin but the darkness provided coverage that would shield anyone from view. Sunrise would cast more light on his search. All he needed to do was keep them safe through the night. Tomorrow, he would assess Gomez's condition and call Gantry to arrange transportation back to base. Whether Hanson would agree to accompany her fellow sergeant was another matter. His past experiences with her had taught him that she would be unlikely to go willingly. The question he asked himself was—could he pull rank on someone he respected so much?

He rechecked all the doors and windows and punched in the intruder alarm code before returning to his post to take up his watch again. A flask of coffee sat by his feet and his gun remained firmly gripped in his hand. He was determined to stand guard until dawn broke through.

Knowing that Cara Hanson had surrendered control to him and finally allowed him to take care of her meant that he could breathe easy at last, if only for a short time.

The early-morning sun fell upon Cara's face, waking her from a deep sleep. She sat up in bed, surprised that she had slept so soundly after the dramatic events of the previous day. She remembered Dean's soft and gentle voice, encouraging her to rest while he took the reins. Just five days ago, she would never have entertained the suggestion. She would have loaded her rifle and insisted on doing the job herself. *But a lot can happen in five days,* she thought to herself.

She knew that Dean, as a Special Forces soldier, was highly trained in close combat, that she was in safe hands. This was the first time she'd allowed herself to truly trust in him, to step back and let him do all the work. This time, she hadn't felt locked away in her room like a naughty child; she'd felt secure and warm, comforted in the knowledge that he was watching over her. She clasped her palm over her forehead in surprise as she realized that she was perilously close to caring about him. Whatever had passed between them in the kitchen had scared her, and she felt herself teetering on the edge of a precipice, knowing that one wrong move could see her falling into a deep chasm of emotional pain. Dean was her commanding officer, and she could not afford to care about him. She could only protect him by keeping a distance between them and treating him like any other assignment. If she hadn't loved her father so very much, she would have stayed calm and controlled. She would've taken a clean shot at that hunter's gun. No, this could not happen again. Never.

She rose from bed and carefully crept out onto the landing, Glock in hand. The door to Dean's bedroom opened as the floorboards creaked, and he stood in the doorway, looking disheveled and tired.

"Good morning, Hanson," he said, smiling. "Did you sleep well?"

"Yeah, I did," she said, nodding. "Best night's sleep in a long time."

He shifted nervously. "Listen, Hanson," he started. "About yesterday in the kitchen…"

She cut him off. "We need to concentrate on the here and now," she said firmly. "I'll go wake Gomez, and the three of us can make a plan together."

She ignored the questioning look in his eyes and went to wake Gomez, determined not to be alone with Dean for long periods again.

In the kitchen, Dean briefed them on the activity he'd witnessed since the sun had risen. He'd spotted two men loitering around the cabin but neither had made a move to attack. One of them held his arm close to his side, as if injured. He'd kept them under surveillance, watching their every step.

"So what do we do now, sir?" asked Gomez. "Do we just wait, like sitting ducks, until they decide to attack?"

"No," said Dean. "I think it's wise for me to continue this mission alone." Cara snapped her eyes up to meet his, but he deftly avoided them. "I'd like to call Gantry and have you both transported back to base. He can put you on lockdown until these terrorists are caught. It's the safest option."

Cara immediately stood and began to pace the room. "You can't do that. You need me, Dean."

He kept his eyes on the floor.

"Look at me, Dean," she pleaded. "You need me."

Gomez's gaze traveled between Cara and Dean. "Why

don't you sleep on it, sir? You look beat. The best decisions are never made in extreme tiredness."

Dean sighed heavily. "Sleep is not an option. I can't leave the cabin guarded by an injured man and a…" He stopped.

Cara's stomach dropped into the floor. She decided to finish his sentence for him. "A woman."

He looked up sharply. All the warm and glowing feelings he'd instilled in her just a few moments ago evaporated in a second. What a fool she'd been to think he was finally beginning to accept her as an equal. He hadn't changed a bit.

"Hanson," he said, leaning over the table toward her. "Can I talk to you in private for a moment?"

She folded her arms. "Anything you have to say, you can say in front of Gomez."

Gomez held up his palms. "Hey, don't drag me into your constant arguments. Sort it out yourselves."

"In the living room please, Sergeant Hanson," Dean said, scraping his chair on the linoleum. "Gomez, keep watch out the window."

Cara swallowed down her fury and followed Dean into the living room, preparing herself for yet another confrontation, yet another blow to her credibility as a soldier. She was so tired of this, of the constant struggle to be accepted. It was draining her of energy.

Dean led her to the couch and sat. She sat on the opposite edge, looking straight ahead, determined not to give him the satisfaction of knowing she was hurting inside.

"I'm sorry, Hanson," he said gently. "But you put those words in my mouth. I never intended to say that."

"That's a lie and you know it." She refused to look in his direction. "You've never seen me as a real soldier. I get it, okay, I'm just a woman, just a feeble, weak, pathetic woman. You don't need to say any more."

She clenched her teeth tight, but she was powerless to prevent the single tear that sprang from her eye and snaked down her face. *How dare you,* she thought to herself, *how dare you make me feel like this.*

She stood up and kept her back to him so he wouldn't see her cry. "Listen," she said, not giving him a chance to speak. "It's clear that you and I will never see eye to eye. But we've got a job to do, and I won't let you stop me from playing my part. You need to sleep. That much is obvious. I am perfectly capable of keeping you safe while you rest, despite only being a woman. If you still want me to leave when you wake up, I won't argue. I'll go willingly. You won't ever have to see me again."

She heard him rise to stand directly behind her. He put his hand on her shoulder.

"I don't feel that way about you, Hanson, I really don't."

The sincerity in his voice choked her. *Don't let him back in, Cara,* she willed herself.

He took a deep breath. "I was going to say that I couldn't leave the cabin guarded by an injured man and a…" He stopped again.

She turned around. "A what?" she challenged.

He swallowed hard and looked at the floor. "A woman I care about."

She took a step backward, uncertain of the meaning behind his words.

"We all care about each other," she said, searching his eyes for signs of the truth within.

"Yes." He nodded, seeming out of breath. "But this is different. It's…" He was struggling to find the right words again. "It's more than that."

Her heartbeat began to thud in her chest. "More? How?"

He moistened his lips. "I don't know. I'm sorry. I shouldn't have said anything. It's nothing. Please forget I ever mentioned it." He was flustered.

"How can I forget it?" she asked, feeling the same sense of dismissal she'd experienced from him too many times before. "This happens every time I want to step up to the plate—you try and stop me and pull me back."

He shook his head and closed his eyes. When he opened them again, he had reverted back to the disciplined commanding officer of old, clearing his throat and standing straight.

"I'll sleep for six hours," he said, without emotion. "You are in command while I rest. Come get me if anything happens." He leaned a little closer. "And I mean anything."

"Yes, sir," she said automatically.

He turned and was gone, leaving her alone to contemplate the enormity of the words he'd never said.

Dean paced the floor of his bedroom, knowing that he wouldn't be able to sleep for some time yet. He squeezed his eyes shut, wishing he could rewind the last half hour of his life and do it all over again. Except, this time, he wouldn't make a total fool of himself in front of his subordinate soldier.

He lay on his bed, staring at the ceiling, willing sleep to come and spare him from this pain. It was better when he simply wanted to protect her as a woman. Now he wanted to protect her as a woman he cared for, a woman who tugged at his heart and, dare he think it, a woman he wanted to be in his life forever.

He got up and began to pace the room again, trying to rid his body of its last remains of energy. A knock at the door stopped him in his tracks and Gomez's voice could be heard on the other side: "Everything okay, sir? There's a lot of movement in there."

"Come in, Gomez," Dean called.

His sergeant entered the room, hobbling on a crutch that Cara had found in the garage. He was delicately balancing a cup of hot tea in his free hand, and it splashed a little on the rug as he walked.

"Let me take that," Dean said, stepping forward and taking the cup. "I assume it's for me."

"It's chamomile," Gomez said. "It might help you sleep. You'll need a clear head later today."

Dean nodded. "I agree. But I think my head is clear enough already."

Gomez looked at the floor. "With all due respect, sir, I think you're allowing your relationship with Sergeant Hanson to affect your state of mind."

Dean stepped back. "You do?"

"I do. It's obvious that you've grown close to her, but you need to keep yourself in check."

Dean adopted a defensive stance. "I'm well aware of my duties, Sergeant, and how to perform them."

Gomez lowered himself into a chair in the corner of the room. "You practically went stir-crazy when Cara stopped calling on her way back from Hurricane. And now you can't sleep. You're thinking about her, am I right?"

Dean didn't answer. He didn't want to lie to one of his soldiers.

Gomez smiled. "I think a good night's sleep will make all the difference to your strength of mind. Try and rest."

Dean took a sip of the tea, accepting that his sergeant was talking sense. If he planned to send Cara back to base when he woke, he'd need all his mental strength. It wasn't going to be easy to banish her from this mission. And from his life.

"I understand your concern," Dean said. "I *am* having trouble sleeping, as it happens. But it's probably just the tension of the mission."

"Yes, sir, it's probably the tension." Gomez reached for his crutch and struggled to stand. Dean went to his side to assist.

"Thanks for the tea," he said. "Just don't tell the troops I drink chamomile, okay?"

"You got it, sir."

When Gomez closed the door behind him, Dean drained his cup and lay on the bed. Try as he might, he couldn't stop his mind returning to Cara. *This is almost over,* he said to himself, *don't flake out now.* He turned onto his side, wishing that the Bible from the kitchen was by his bedside. He'd obviously upset Cara with his words earlier, making her feel inadequate. He wanted to go to her and apologize and tell her that he would never knowingly do anything to hurt her. But Gomez was right. He needed to put some emotional distance between them.

In his weaker moments, he'd wondered what it would feel like to share more than a professional life with Cara. But the thought left him almost breathless with fear. He'd never felt this out of control in his life, not even during his father's most violent attacks. At least his mother was safe now, knowing that her ex-husband was in jail. The threat in her life had been eliminated, but the danger in Cara's life would remain ever present, as long as she served in the U.S. Army, always under threat from the enemy's long reach. He couldn't go back to living with that fear in his life, dreading the day when the worst would happen. No matter how much he cared for Cara, he wouldn't allow that feeling to destroy him again. His only option was to get as far away from her as he possibly could and spare himself the torment.

* * *

Cara set up her position in an upstairs bedroom. She opened the window just the tiniest of cracks and slid the end of her rifle outside. There was no chance of using the prone position, but she'd made herself as comfortable as possible while sitting upright, using her tripod to support the long barrel of her M29 sniper rifle. She'd owned this rifle for so long, it often felt like an extra limb. She felt melded with it.

Gomez was keeping watch downstairs, and she was satisfied they had all bases covered. She was still smarting from Dean's comments about her ability to guard the cabin. He had hurt her deeply this time, and she felt unable to simply brush it off. She would never prove herself to him, no matter what.

Movement in the undergrowth caught her attention. She froze, then brought her face, ever so slowly, to the telescopic sight of her rifle. She watched a figure moving quietly through the trees in the small woodland just a few hundred yards away. He was dressed entirely in black with a ski mask covering his face. He moved like a soldier, expertly darting from tree to tree, keeping his left arm pulled close to his body. In his right hand, he carried a black pistol, which she suspected was a U.S. Military, standard-issue Beretta. Attached to its barrel was a long, sleek suppressor. Whoever this was, he wanted to do the job as quietly as possible. He was gaining good ground, coming increasingly closer to the cabin. She gathered her thoughts, remembering that Dean had instructed her to wake him at the first sign of attack. She deliberated for a second or two and decided against it. She was more than capable of dealing with this situation, despite his lack of confidence in her. She had the man in her sights and, she concluded, she would take him down—just a leg shot, enough to incapacitate him. Only when she had subdued him, would she wake Dean.

Then she saw another man. He appeared as if from nowhere, running soundlessly toward the man in black. He was wearing combat pants and a hooded sweatshirt, pulled up tightly over his head, although she could just make out the bold red color of a bandanna underneath. She gasped, realizing that this was the sniper from the hill. She watched as he tackled the man in black to the ground, holding him in a headlock. What on earth was going on? These men were sent to attack *them,* weren't they, not each other? The man in black flailed and struggled under the grip of the large bulk of the stronger man. The figure in the bandanna then produced a syringe from his pocket and jabbed it firmly into the neck of his victim, holding him tightly in his grasp as he slumped forward to lie motionless on the wet leaves.

Then she watched the lone man move quicker than ever, running toward the cabin, setting her heart racing as she reassessed what to do. She decided quickly. She would take down this target, instead, preventing him from reaching their door and breaking through. It was her fault that danger had found them, her fault that Dean was within its grasp, and *she* would neutralize the threat.

She lined up her leg shot, noting that he was wearing a bulletproof vest. He'd come prepared. "Nice and slow," she murmured to herself. "Just a bit closer." She curled her finger around the trigger, satisfied that her shot was perfect. She fired! The man sank into the leaves, but he instantly jumped up and continued running, having been startled by the shot but obviously not directly hit. No! How could that be? She'd missed! She shook her head in disbelief. She'd missed a clean shot! That was impossible. She gathered her thoughts again and leaned back to the telescopic sight of her rifle to take another attempt. He'd vanished. She felt panic rise in her chest. Where had he gone? It didn't take long for the answer to come, as she heard a commotion downstairs. Gomez! She flew from her chair and raced to the stairs, taking them two at a time to rush to the aid of her fellow soldier in his time of need.

She reached the foot of the stairs to see Gomez bravely fighting to hold the front door against powerful blows being rained upon it from the outside. With each thud, the wood splintered and buckled. She pulled her handgun from its holster and darted to the window to see the man in the bandanna using his powerful legs to bring the door close to breaking off its hinges. Gomez's weakened state was no match for the strength he was pitted against. Her mind raced with possibilities. Surely, Dean would hear the commotion and come to their aid. Why hadn't she woken him at the first sign of danger as he'd asked?

"Gomez," she cried out. "Stand back. Let him come in and we'll take him down together. Aim for the legs."

"My gun," Gomez replied through gritted teeth. "It's been knocked out of my hand by the impact."

She searched the floor for signs of his weapon, catching sight of it resting just underneath the leg of the couch. She dashed to retrieve it. Too late! The door crashed open, sending Gomez sprawling across the carpet with a yelp.

She turned on her heel, raising her weapon to fire, but he was on her in an instant. She saw a flash of red as the man in the bandanna swept her off her feet, holding her tight and paralyzing her with his power. She kicked and struggled and tried to shout for Dean, but a hand clamped over her mouth, leaving her struggling for breath. Gomez was lying prone on the floor, clutching his leg, writhing in agony. Her gun was snatched from her hand and tucked into the waistband of the man's baggy pants.

Her muffled cries were caught on the wind as she was carried out into the late-afternoon air and down the lane to a small blue compact car parked on the road, cleverly placed to be out of sight from the cabin. She was bundled into the trunk and the man stood over her, keeping her firmly pressed to the rough carpet lining the small space. He leaned close to her face and pulled down the hood on his sweatshirt.

"I'm sorry that I have to do this," he said. "But Dean will save you. All you have to do is wait."

She looked up at him. Where had she seen that same long face and Roman nose? She searched her memory. Yes, it was the same face from the photograph she'd been given on that first day of their mission.

"Major Moore?" she gasped.

"Don't believe everything you've been told about me," he said, before closing the trunk and covering her in darkness.

She kicked out against the confinement. Boy, she'd *really* messed up this time. As the seconds ticked by, she imagined Dean being dragged from his bed. She listened for the sound of a gunshot—thankfully none came. When the engine started up and the car pulled out onto the road, she realized that she was being taken hostage. Had Dean possibly escaped the cabin, and now Moore was using her as bait to lure him out of his hiding place? Would Moore demand a ransom to fund the terrorist organization he supported? Only time would tell what fate awaited her.

"Stupid, stupid, stupid!" she shouted at herself in the darkness. All her fears had been realized in this moment, and she had failed in the most gargantuan way. Dean was better off without her, and she hoped he wouldn't rush to save her. She hoped he would abandon her to her fate and wash his hands of her ineptness. But as his face settled on her mind, she knew he would come for her. Her heart told her so.

* * *

Dean sat up and checked his watch. Seven hours had passed and no one had woken him. He'd slept more heavily than usual and he was groggy, as if he'd been drugged. But that was impossible, wasn't it?

He rose and walked to the window, opening the drapes a little and looking outside. His eyes widened as he saw a figure lying facedown in the leaves at the front of the cabin. By his side was a pistol, adorned with a powerful silencer.

Dean grabbed his gun and ran from the room, hurling himself down the stairs to find Gomez tied to a chair, his head bent forward onto his chest.

"Hanson," Dean called out. A pain started to build in his chest. "Hanson!"

Gomez's head sprang up, and he mumbled through the rag in his mouth. Dean pulled the fabric from between his teeth and quickly freed him.

"Moore's got Hanson," Gomez said, rubbing his leg. "I'm sorry, sir, I couldn't stop him. They left a couple of hours ago."

"How did I miss this?" Dean shouted, more at himself than at Gomez. "I was just upstairs."

Gomez closed his eyes and circled his temples. "I'm sorry, sir. I saw how much you needed to sleep, so I slipped a sedative into your tea last night."

"You *what?*"

Gomez held up his palms. "I was worried about you. I've seen what sleep deprivation does to the mind."

"That was not your call to make, Gomez." Dean paced as he spoke. "I can't believe you did something so irresponsible."

"I only put in a small amount. I thought it would have a mild effect."

Dean clenched his hands into fists. Gomez had prevented him from protecting Cara when she needed him. Now she was gone and he was powerless to reach her, to stop a hand from striking her, hurting her in ways he didn't want to imagine.

"We're wasting time," Dean said. "We should be looking for her." He exhaled loudly. He didn't even know where to start.

"Moore put this in my hand," Gomez said, holding a piece of paper aloft. "He told me you'd understand what it means."

Dean took the paper from the sergeant's hand and looked at the writing on it: *Psalm 81.* He moved quickly to the kitchen and retrieved the Bible from the counter, leafing through the pages as he walked back to Gomez.

He read the words of the psalm. "*I answered thee in the secret place of Thunder.*"

Gomez looked blankly at him. "What does it mean, sir?"

"It's a place Chris and I used to go fishing. Thunder Lodge in Colorado. It's a message only I would understand. He's telling me to go to our fishing spot near Thunder Lodge."

Gomez stood on his one good leg. "Then what are we waiting for? Let's go."

"I'll take you to the hospital first," Dean said. "Then I'll go alone."

Gomez hobbled to his crutch. "I'd appreciate the opportunity to make things right, sir. Let me do what I can. Please."

Dean didn't have the time to argue. "Okay. But this is personal. Moore wants me, so you stay out of sight."

He dropped the paper and holstered his gun. As the paper fluttered to the ground, he saw more words written on the back: *Don't be followed.*

Dean took Gomez's arm around his shoulder and led him to the SUV, helping him inside. The man in the black ski mask was rousing from whatever had felled him. He stood up in the leaves, staggering slightly. He caught Dean in his sights and set off running toward him, aiming his pistol to shoot. Dean jumped into the driver's seat and sped away as shots rang out behind him. He kept the man in his rearview mirror, watching him race after the car. Dean drove to the end of the lane, stopping briefly to open the car window and shoot a perfect hole in a tire of the battered, silver sedan.

Then he turned his thoughts to Cara. She had been the one who'd wanted to believe in the goodness of Chris Moore, the one who'd wanted to give him a chance of redemption. Now, Chris had revealed his true colors by overpowering an injured man and taking a woman half his size as a prisoner. What kind of man behaved like this? Certainly not the man Chris used to be. Dean hardened his heart again, angry for daring to believe that his old friend had been trying to help them. This time Chris would not escape his punishment. If he had harmed a single hair upon Cara's head he would pay a heavy price.

Please God, he thought silently, *stand guard over her until I can take over.*

TEN

Cara felt herself bouncing along a stony track. She estimated that she'd been in the car for over six hours, and her back was stiff and sore. She'd used the time to pray, not for herself but for Dean. She knew he would blame himself for her failings, assuming it was his fault for not keeping her safe. Now she would have to accept that any credibility she'd had as a soldier would be well and truly gone. If she couldn't even save herself from harm, what chance did she have of saving others? She buried her head in her hands, the reputation that she'd worked so hard to build over the last seven years crumbling to dust.

The air outside was cold and brisk. She felt it whistle through the cracks in the trunk, and she began to shake uncontrollably. She fought hard to suppress the fear that bubbled up in her stomach as it moved all the way to her chest and into her mouth. This was by far the most dangerous situation she'd ever found herself in, and she had no experience of how to react. No training had prepared her for this. She shivered against the deepening wind outside, imagining the sky growing dark and the terrain growing remote. Without her weapon, she was utterly defenseless, at the mercy of whatever situation awaited her. She squeezed her eyes tightly shut, bitterly regretting ever encouraging

Dean to trust in Moore. He'd blindsided her, and she'd walked right into his trap. Could scripture really have led her to this desolate place?

The car came to a stop, and she heard the driver's door being slammed. She braced herself for the release of the trunk and, when it popped open, she kicked out with all the force she could muster. Major Moore cried out as she planted a quick, glancing blow on his chin. She sprang up from her position and leaped like an alley cat from the confined space, landing on the rocky ground with a crunch. She pushed herself up to run, but cramp set in where her muscles had been curled up tight for too long. She fell to her knees before pulling herself up again, determined to get as far away as she could. Then she felt herself in the air, swept off her feet by two strong arms. She grabbed one of the arms and sank her teeth into the flesh, feeling a taste of blood seep into her mouth.

Moore didn't even flinch. "I heard you were feisty, but I never expected you to be so strong."

Major Moore carried her along a dead-end track, leading to a small, stone building at the end. Now she had the opportunity to look around, she could see that this place was deserted—a wide-open landscape with a flat, calm lake right in the center.

"I'll kill you as soon as I get the chance," she spat, feeling his arms tighten their grip to contain her flailing limbs.

He laughed. "I can see why Dean likes you. You're tough like him."

"How would you know?" she challenged. "You don't know me."

"I've been watching you for days," he said, "making sure that the UFA can't get to you. You and Dean work well together. I see something special between you. If I know Dean McGovern as well as I think I do, he'll come for you."

"Don't bank on it," she bluffed as they entered the dark interior of the stone shelter. "I told him never to risk his life for me."

He put her on her feet and stood in the doorway, blocking her exit.

"I see you like him, too," he said, smiling. "He'll come for you, all right. I'm counting on it."

Dean kept his foot pressed hard to the accelerator, willing the damaged SUV to go faster. He was almost there, almost within reach of Cara. He'd counted down the minutes as they turned into long, dragging hours. Eight hours had passed since she'd gone. Anything could've happened in that time. He could sense her closeness.

"Hang on," he whispered under his breath, "just hang on."

Gomez turned his head. "I take it you're not talking to me, sir?"

"You stay in the car, Gomez," Dean said, seeing a small blue compact come into view on the rocky path. "Keep your gun close, stay alert. If anything happens to me, get Hanson out of here. Do whatever it takes but get her to safety, okay?"

"Understood, sir. My leg's pretty messed up, but I can still shoot a gun and drive a car. If she needs me, I'll do whatever I can to get her back to base. It's the least I can do."

Dean patted Gomez on the shoulder and exited the car, holding his gun to his side, walking down the path to the small stone shelter where he and Chris spent many days fishing in happier times. Daylight had faded entirely and he peered into the moonlit terrain. Then he saw Chris standing at the water's edge, holding Cara tightly to his chest, a gun pointed at her head.

"No!" Dean called instinctively, holding out a hand to stop Chris from carrying out his threat. "Please, Chris, don't hurt her. She's innocent in all this. It's not her you want, it's me. Let her go and I'll die in her place."

He very slowly crouched to the ground and laid his gun on the stones. Then he stood upright and held out his hands, palms forward.

"I have no other weapons, I assure you." He looked at Cara's face. She didn't seem scared. She seemed to be *smiling*.

"You okay, Cara?" he asked. It no longer seemed appropriate to call her Hanson. She meant more than that to him.

"I'm fine," she called. "He didn't hurt me. He's given me food and water."

Dean exhaled as relief surged through him.

"Dean, all I want to do is talk," Chris called. "I don't want anyone to die, least of all my best friend. I'm the same man who spent all those days fishing with you here just a year ago." He removed the gun from Cara's temple and held it midair. "I'm going to place this gun on the ground and we can talk, okay? You have my word that I won't hurt anyone."

Dean nodded but decided to remain on his guard nonetheless.

Chris released his grip on Cara and placed his gun on the ground. She stood motionless for a few seconds before running into Dean's embrace, wrapping her arms tightly around his neck, burying her face in the dip of his shoulder. He held her close, breathing in the scent from her hair, thanking God for keeping her safe until he found her.

"Thank you," she whispered into his ear.

"I had to come for you," he whispered back.

She pulled back slightly and looked into his eyes. "I'm not thanking you for coming for me. I'm thanking you for offering to die for me."

She brought her hand up to his face and brushed his cheek, before placing a kiss, very lightly, on his lips. The jolt through his body took his breath away and he momentarily forgot where he was. Her soft, warm lips took him to a place far away from there—a place of perfect respite from the weariness he felt inside. Then it was gone. It was so fleeting that he wondered if it had been real at all.

She pulled away from his arms and stood beside him, reaching down and lacing her fingers through his.

"He was kind to me," she said. "He says he just wants us to listen to what he has to say. Whether we trust him or not is a decision we make together."

He nodded, breathing deeply to bring his senses back into the here and now.

They walked together to where Chris stood by the water.

"I'm sorry, Sergeant Hanson," Chris said. "I know this experience will have frightened you, but there was no other way I could reach Dean. Please forgive me."

Dean stepped in front of Cara and placed himself between her and Chris. "I heard that you intend to kill me. Is that why you lured me here? Is that why you took Cara, to use her as bait?"

"I've been trying to reach you for months, Dean," Chris said. "Every time I get a message out, it's intercepted and destroyed by the mole in Special Forces. The only way I could think of to reach you, without the UFA knowing, was by using scripture. It's something we both trust, right?"

"But why bring me all the way out here?" Dean said, anxiously scanning the surrounding terrain for signs of any accomplices. "I was right there in the cabin." He felt Cara hook her finger through his belt loop. "You didn't need to kidnap the only woman I've ever…" He stopped. "The only woman I've ever had in my team."

"I had to get you out of the danger zone," Moore said. "You're being watched constantly, and I couldn't risk having this talk in a place where we're all prime targets. I injected a tranquilizer into the guy who was staking out your cabin, but I wasn't sure how long it would last. I needed to bring you to a safe and quiet place where the enemy can't reach us."

Dean raised his index finger. "*You* are the enemy."

"No," Chris said, "I've been set up. After going undercover in the UFA I got real close to finding the mole in Special Forces, the one who smuggled the bomb into Fort Bragg. I narrowed it down to someone in Tenth Group and I was about to uncover the truth when the mole found out about me. The UFA decided to make me their fall guy and they falsified paperwork implicating *me* as the traitor in Tenth Group. That meant the real culprit could carry on undetected and I became public enemy number one. I had no choice but to go on the run and try to contact you, knowing that you were the one person who'd believe me."

"How do you know I believe you?"

"Because I asked God to lead me to you." He smiled. "And it worked, didn't it?"

Dean thought of the trail of scripture that had led them to that point. "It worked," he admitted.

"I've been watching over you for days," Chris said, "ever since the bomb in the mountains forced you on the run. The UFA has been watching you, too, waiting to strike. It was a race against time to get to you before they did."

Dean folded his arms. "Is it true that I'm on their hit list?"

"Yes, Dean," Chris confirmed. "They wanted to terminate you before I could get to you and tell you the truth. They'll be looking to take both of us out now. We know too much."

Dean nodded and placed a hand on his friend's shoulder. "Thank you, Chris," he said as the knot in his stomach gave way to a more peaceful sensation. "Thank you for keeping us safe."

"Wait a minute." Cara stepped forward. She pointed at Chris. "*You* were the sniper I saw in the hills. *You* were the one shooting at Dean."

Dean took a step back and pulled Cara to his side. "Is that true?"

"Yes," Chris said, "but I wasn't shooting to hurt you. I was shooting to warn you. I knew you were walking into a trap. I thought I could get you to abort the mission if I could hit the ground right by you. I knew they were trying to lure you toward the bomb. I didn't know what else to do."

Dean ran a hand down his face. "You have no idea how complicated this all is," he said. "You need to speak to Colonel Gantry. There's a lot more to this story than you realize."

Chris looked between Dean and Cara. "Does this mean you believe me? You trust me?"

"I guess it all makes sense," said Dean. "Cara said it was a sloppy sniper with no camouflage cover." He looked at Chris, trying to rebuild the broken bond between them and allow himself to trust again. "You never were an organized marksman."

"No," Chris said as a smile spread over his face. "I never had the patience to be a sniper. Not like Hanson here—she's an amazing shooter."

"I missed *you* though, didn't I?" she said.

Chris raised his eyebrows up high. "You sure about that, Sergeant?"

"Yeah," she said. "I was trying to take a leg shot, but the bullet hit the ground, instead."

Chris pulled the material on the leg of his khaki pants out wide. "I think you'll find the serious bruise on my thigh tells a different story."

Cara's gaze traveled to the fabric, pulled taut, in Chris's hand, and she gasped as the small hole became apparent, revealing a thick, protective barrier beneath.

"Bullet-resistant body armor," Chris explained, turning to Dean. "Having seen the skills of this sniper, I knew I couldn't afford to take any chances. She could take me down before I even blinked." He laughed. "You have no idea how uncomfortable it is wearing a full body kit, but I was forced to take every precaution."

Dean looked at Cara, who was gazing in wonderment at the perfect bullet hole in Chris's pants leg.

"So I didn't miss?" she said, dropping her jaw at the revelation that her accuracy had been dead straight.

"No, Sergeant, you didn't miss," Chris said, clasping her shoulder. "It was a faultless shot."

Dean saw a look of pride sweep over Cara's face. Her biggest fear had not been realized. She'd made the shot and her aim had been true. He smiled at her, knowing that they both understood the significance of why this news meant so much.

Dean took Cara by the arm and turned her away from Chris. "Cara and I need to talk in private," he said, leading her farther along the water's edge. Once out of earshot, he whispered to her. "His story all seems to add up, but we agreed to make this decision together. If you don't trust him, we'll walk away. You seem to have good instincts about people. What do you think?"

She glanced at Chris. "I trust him."

Dean smiled, finally allowing the anxiety weighing on his mind to dissipate. "Good," he said. "I was hoping you'd say that."

Dean walked toward his friend with a new spring in his step. He stood in front of Chris and held out his hand. "Welcome back, buddy."

Chris ignored the hand, and gave his old comrade a bear hug, slapping him on the back as he released him. "It's good to be back, partner."

Chris's eyes flickered over to Cara. "I can see a lot has changed since I've been gone. You replaced me with someone who's as hot-tempered as you."

Dean smiled. "She's a better shot, too."

Chris nodded his head. "And a lot easier on the eyes."

Cara stepped forward. "Careful there, Major. As you know, my bite is a lot worse than my bark." She held out her hand, looking at him sternly. "Can I have my weapon back, please?"

Chris pulled her Glock 17 from his waistband, handing it to her, handle forward. He sidled over to Dean, speaking out the corner of his mouth.

"Wow! I never knew there was a woman who could take you down."

"Quit joking, Chris," Dean said, slipping easily back into their familiar banter. "She hasn't taken me down."

Chris laughed heartily. Cara looked up from where she was checking her weapon. "What's so funny?"

"Nothing, Sergeant," Chris said, beginning to walk up the stone track back to the car. "My old friend here was just trying to convince me that he's the same man he used to be."

"He isn't?" asked Cara.

"No way," said Chris, ignoring Dean's narrowed eyes,

warning him off. "For a start, he put down his weapon and laid himself wide open. No soldier would do that, especially one trained in Special Forces."

"But he did it to save me," Cara said. "He's my commanding officer."

"Yeah," Chris called back. "But show me a soldier who'd take that kind of risk. With no means of defense, it means you both die."

Dean quickened his pace to catch up with Chris, flicking his ear as he reached his side. "Cut it out," he said. "I know what you're doing."

He checked behind to see Cara jogging up the path to join them. She caught his gaze and he looked away, suddenly feeling the need to reinforce his emotional distance.

"He's a good soldier," Cara said to Chris, "doing what he needs to protect his team."

Chris glanced over to Dean and grinned widely. He kept his voice low, just loud enough for his friend to hear. "I don't think he was being a soldier at all. I think he was being a man."

As the sun broke through a cold, Colorado morning, Colonel Gantry leaned back on a picnic table with a solemn expression on his face. With Dean and Cara standing nearby, Gantry had just listened to Chris speaking for over an hour, paying close attention and nodding, but never interrupting. He allowed his subordinate soldier to finish his long and complicated story before speaking.

"So what you're saying is that we have a traitor in Tenth Group?"

Chris nodded. "Yes, sir."

"But you don't know who?"

"No, sir, not yet, but I'm working on it."

Gantry took off his hat and scratched his forehead,

looking around the public park surrounding them, no doubt wondering if they were being watched at that very moment.

Chris picked at the wood splinters on the picnic table where they sat. "Dean has updated me on your awareness of the bomb and plan of attack," he said, bowing his head. "I'm sorry, sir. If I'd had any idea that you had the situation under control, I would never have tried to warn Dean off. I realize I made a bad situation a whole lot worse."

Gantry exhaled loudly. "Yes, you did, Major, but I understand why you did it. This mission was always going to be messy, and you can't be blamed for that." He looked into the distance. "Sergeant Hicks paid a heavy price for our mistakes." He sighed deeply. "The blame for that is mine alone—the buck stops with me."

Gantry looked at Cara standing at the head of the table, prowling back and forth, her hand resting on the weapon she had concealed beneath her shirt. Dean was operating like a bookend on the other side, and together they had formed a protective ring around the colonel and major while they talked.

"Do you support Major Moore's story, Sergeant Hanson?" Gantry asked.

She stopped pacing and stood erect. "Yes, sir, I do. Captain McGovern and I have total faith in his allegiance to you and the U.S. Military."

She looked at Chris Moore and smiled. In the car, they had all talked at length about everything that had happened. Chris had spoken honestly and open-heartedly about the six months he had spent trying to send a message to Dean. He'd slept out in the open, living under the radar, putting his faith in God and never doubting his belief that the truth would prevail. He was a good man, and Dean was clearly overjoyed to have him back. She felt gladness in her heart—gladness tinged with regret. Since kissing Dean at Thunder Lodge, he had been avoiding her gaze, probably embarrassed by her typically feminine display of emotion. She'd dropped her guard for a split second and revealed her secret self, the one normally kept buried deep beneath khakis and camouflage.

Gantry turned to Dean, who confirmed Cara's words without looking in her direction.

"We'll find out who did this, sir," Dean said. "Hicks's death won't go unpunished."

"But time is running out, Captain," Gantry said. "We know another attack is coming and we need a resolution."

Chris leaned toward Gantry. "One thing is certain. I know too much now. I can identify too many of the UFA leaders. They're very secretive, but I've seen a few of their faces. They'll be gunning for me, and I won't be safe at Fort Carson." He looked up into the misty sky. "I'll stay off radar and wait for them to come to me. Whatever happens, I'm better off alone."

Dean stepped forward. "Nobody's better off alone." His eyes flicked to Cara's for a tiny moment. "You're safer in a team. I'll stay with you."

Cara watched Dean place his hand on his friend's shoulder and she, too, stepped forward. "I'll stay, too. You could use a sniper watching over you."

She saw it again: the cheek twitch, but she didn't feel angry or annoyed. She knew that Dean's desire to protect her came from a place of goodness, and she tried not to judge him too harshly for it. He was a product of his past, just like her. And he finally seemed to be making good on his promise to try to change. This time he didn't try to talk her out of it, even though she suspected he wished he could.

Gantry rose from the table. "I won't even try to change

your mind, Sergeant Hanson. You and Captain McGovern are like peas in a pod, both as forceful and stubborn as each other."

Dean looked at the ground. She saw color creep into his cheeks, and he turned to the rolling, green landscape as his shoulders rose and fell with deep breaths. She felt her own breathing grow stronger in response. She had never considered that their similarities were so obvious to others.

Gantry put his hat back on and saluted his men. "Good luck, soldiers," he said. "I commend you for your dedication to defeating the menace that has infiltrated the safety of the U.S. Military." He reached round to the back of his waistband and unclipped a small radio. He handed it to Chris. "Keep this radio tuned to channel nine—it's a direct comms line to the Utah National Guard at Camp Williams. I'll make sure the Nineteenth Airborne Group is on standby. If you can't do this alone, call them immediately."

Chris took the radio. "If we call the National Guard, sir, the terrorists will go to ground again. We stand a better chance of luring them out by remaining small in number."

"Of course," replied Gantry solemnly, "but I don't want to lose any of you. Your lives are more important than theirs."

Gantry turned to walk toward his jeep, parked next to their SUV, newly patched up by a young corporal accompanying the colonel. He'd worked on it while the soldiers talked, repairing the headlight and hammering out the crumpled hood. From a distance, it looked as good as new.

"We've done the best repairs possible with your vehicle," the colonel said. "But I understand it's an enemy car, so it'll be highly visible to them."

Dean ran his hand over the dimpled metal of the SUV's wing. "Cara was run off the road after she took a visit to Hurricane and she could only escape by taking their vehicle. She thinks she may have met her attacker before, but his face was hidden so she can't be sure."

"Oh, I've met him before," Cara said. "I know I have." She delved into the recesses of her mind to try and pinpoint where she had seen his wiry figure. But she came up blank.

"It's a Texas plate," Gantry observed. "Did you check who it's registered to?"

"I tried," Dean replied. "But someone hacked into the state records and covered their tracks. I've got an IT technician working on it."

Gantry looked at the SUV and then at his own army jeep. "Would you like to swap vehicles with me? I can take the SUV for forensic analysis."

Dean held up his hand. "I'd rather keep it for a while longer, sir. I *want* the enemy to find us. I want to finish this."

Cara straightened her back. "So do I."

"That makes three of us," Chris said, putting his arms around both Dean and Cara. "But what about Gomez?"

Gomez sat in the front seat of the SUV, cradling his leg, which had been further damaged by the events of the day. The pain was clearly etched on his face but he hadn't complained once. Gantry opened the door of the car.

"Sergeant Gomez, I strongly advise you to return to Fort Carson with me. That leg needs immediate attention."

Gomez cast his eyes over his three colleagues. "I'm sorry to bail, guys, but I'm no good to you like this. I'd just slow you down."

Dean nodded and walked to the car door to help the injured man from the vehicle. "Careful now, Gomez," he said. "Make sure you rest and get well. Special Forces can manage without you for a while."

Gomez smiled. "Thank you, sir." He hopped out of the

car and leaned against the side, looking over in Cara's direction. "Do you think I could talk to Sergeant Hanson for a minute?" he asked. "In private."

Dean exchanged glances with Cara and gave a quick nod of the head. "You've got two minutes, Gomez. Make it brief."

The men stepped away from the car, and Cara approached Gomez, noticing that he was shifting uncomfortably on his one good leg. She went to his side and allowed him to lean on her shoulder.

"Sergeant Hanson," he began, "I owe you an apology."

The shock on her face must have been clearly visible.

"Yeah, I know," he continued, "I'm not one for apologies normally, but I didn't give you a chance when we started this mission, and I was hard on you. You're an awesome soldier, Sergeant, and if I ever go into combat again, I'd be happy to fight alongside you."

She felt tears prick her eyes. She'd never received this kind of affirmation from a male counterpart before. She blinked the moisture away quickly, hoping he hadn't noticed her sentimental response to his praise.

"Thank you, Gomez," she said, giving him a brief hug. "That means a lot coming from you."

She helped him hobble to Colonel Gantry's jeep. "Keep the captain safe now," Gomez said, lowering himself gingerly into the passenger seat. "He needs someone watching his back."

"I will." She glanced over to Dean, who was watching her and Gomez with his arms crossed, his expression showing signs of tension.

Whatever mistakes she had made, whatever Dean felt about her emotional state, she would protect him to the best of her ability and not rest until the job was done. Only then would she retreat from his life, allowing him

to return to the uncomplicated world of Special Forces—a
male-dominated world, which she could never infiltrate.
She knew he'd tried hard to accept her as an equal, and
she was grateful for that, but it wasn't enough. She needed
more from a commanding officer. And, she realized, she
needed more from a man.

ELEVEN

Dean drove through the misty morning as Chris slept in the seat beside him, and Cara slept across the seat in the back. He felt apprehensive, uncertain of what they would face when they arrived back at the cabin, but they had collectively decided to face the enemy head-on. Whatever Sergeant Gomez had said to Cara had given her expression a new sense of pride, hopefully easing the guilt she felt for putting his own life in danger.

He'd wanted to tell her that he didn't blame her. He'd wanted to tell her that he was proud of her and that she had proven herself beyond all doubt in his mind. Chris had told him how hard she'd fought against him, battling like a tigress protecting her cubs. His mother used to fight the same way, standing in front of him and his sister, acting as a barrier against the whisky-fueled temper of his father. He'd been terrified of his dad when he was small, but something about his mom's fierceness had comforted him and reassured him that she would keep them safe. He struggled to pinpoint when it had all changed—the point when his mother had given up the fight and resigned herself to her situation. That was the moment he'd stepped up, despite only being twelve years old. When his mom had been beaten into submission, he took the reins, switching places with her without a moment's hesitation. It had seemed as natural as breathing. But, he reminded himself, she had once been a strong and feisty woman, a fighter like Cara. Did he really want Cara Hanson to submit to a man's authority like his mother had done with his father?

He shook the thought away, as though even thinking it was incomprehensible. Despite the pain it caused him, he knew he had to let her spirit fly to places that his protective shield couldn't reach.

Chris stirred in the seat next to him. He rubbed his eyes. "Best sleep I've had in six months." He grinned, glancing to the seat behind him. "Sleeping like a princess."

Dean smiled. "Don't ever call her that," he advised. "She'll floor you. Not with her fists but with her words."

Chris laughed softly. "You two are close, huh?"

Dean looked at his friend from the corner of his eye. "She's my subordinate," he said. "It's my job to get close to all my soldiers."

"Is it your job to *kiss* all your soldiers?" Chris said, moving his posture to gauge Dean's reaction. "Because I didn't get that memo."

"*She* kissed *me*."

"Oh, I see," Chris said with teasing sarcasm. "I could tell that you didn't enjoy it. It must've been horrible to have a beautiful woman in your arms, kissing you like that."

"Quit it, Major."

Chris widened his eyes, feigning innocence. "I'm just telling it like it is, buddy. I've known you a long time, and I've never seen you like this."

"Like what?"

"Do I have to spell it out for you? Like a man in love."

Dean snorted in reply. "I'm not in love with her. I've only known her six days."

Chris raised his palms. "That's all it takes."

Dean felt a knot growing in his stomach. He glanced behind to check that Cara was still asleep. He didn't want her hearing this conversation. In truth, he didn't want to be having this conversation at all.

Chris drew a breath. "Have you prayed about it?"

Dean closed his eyes, just for a moment. "No."

"Why not? I left you a Bible, didn't I?"

"It's not God's job to sort out my love life," he said, quickly regretting the words he'd chosen to use. Cara wasn't part of his love life. He didn't even have a love life.

Chris rubbed his temples. "I can see that a lot has changed since I've been gone. It may not be God's job to sort out your love life, but He wants to point you in the right direction. The rest is up to you."

"This is all irrelevant," Dean said, as his patience gave way to irritation. "Cara's life is in the Fifth Infantry. She's a sniper. It kills me knowing that she will walk into danger every day of her life." He shook his head. "I couldn't live with that kind of worry."

Chris lowered his gravelly voice. "Plenty of military wives live with that kind of worry every day, but they cope with it. They suck it up and carry on. It's no different for men whose wives are actively serving." He leaned over a little. "We all have to make sacrifices to be with the one we love."

"Not me," Dean said. "I can't make that kind of sacrifice."

Chris leaned back in his seat. "Okay," he said. "I guess you can wait until you find another woman who's perfect for you."

"Who said she was perfect for me?"

"You did."

"Shut up," Dean said playfully.

Chris's face changed from jokey to grave in a second.

"Seriously, buddy. Wouldn't you rather spend just one day with Cara Hanson than a whole lifetime alone?"

Dean drew a quick breath and his palms grew moist on the wheel. "Let's drop it. You've been on your own too much. You don't know when to stop talking."

"All I'm saying…"

"I said *drop it.*"

Chris nodded. "Okay, okay."

Dean rolled his shoulders, trying to rid his body of the tension that had built up in his muscles. He shook away the ridiculous suggestion that he was in love with Cara. Yes, he cared for her and wanted to keep her safe, but he certainly wasn't in love with her. He was immune to love, wasn't he? Yet he couldn't stop his eyes from traveling to the rearview mirror to watch her sleeping, stretched out on the seat. She was lying in the fetal position with her hand tucked underneath her head, resting on her cheek. The other hand was on her gun, her fingers lightly curled around the dark handle. Her blond hair fell across the seat in a cascade of gold, and her face was the most perfect picture of peace he had ever seen.

He took his gaze back to the road as an unwelcome sensation gripped him. He sensed she was in danger, and the vision of her bleeding in his arms returned to him. Worst of all, he knew he was powerless to prevent it.

The misty morning had given way to a clear, sunny day as the cabin came into view. Cara was grateful that she had slept for the entire journey, allowing her to recharge her batteries for the day ahead. Dean and Chris had shared the driving, choosing not to wake her. As a sniper, it was vital that her senses were clear and sharp, and they knew she could be the key to their survival.

Dean navigated the driveway with caution. The battered silver sedan was still parked on the road with a perfectly flat tire. There was no sign of anyone entering the cabin and no evidence of booby traps. They proceeded with care, exiting the vehicle with weapons drawn. It was all clear.

Chris laughed nervously. "They probably never thought we'd be so stupid as to come back."

"It's not stupid to come back," Cara said. "In a fight for survival, the winners are always those who know the terrain the best."

She looked into the distance. She knew practically every brook, tree and shrub for miles around. No one could outwit her here.

Dean checked the door for traps and walked through the cabin, making sure it was safe. He came out with a smile on his face.

"All clear," he said. "Let's get inside and eat. I'm starving."

Dean started making breakfast while Cara returned to her lookout position upstairs. Her rifle was still resting on the windowpane where she had abandoned it to rush to the aid of Sergeant Gomez. It had slid from the wooden frame and was hanging limply on its tripod. She repositioned it, and sat down to play the waiting game, slipping effortlessly into the routine she'd adopted hundreds of times before.

She was still embarrassed by her display of affection toward Dean the previous day and desperately hoped he wouldn't mention it. She'd allowed her emotions to get the better of her and had, momentarily, dropped the tough exterior that she always presented in her job. The cold, clinical training of sniper school had not prepared her for matters of the heart.

Renewing her vow to keep Dean safe, she brought her

binoculars to her eyes and combed every inch of the woodland, certain that nothing and no one would escape her sight. She became so engrossed in her task that his entrance into the room startled her. She jumped from her chair.

"Sorry, Sergeant," he said. "I didn't mean to scare you."

She noticed that he had reverted to calling her *sergeant*. She rebuked herself when her heart sank a little. *He's your commanding officer,* she thought silently, *and you are his sergeant.*

"Anything to report, sir?" she asked. She decided that she, too, would lapse into formal terms of address.

"No, not yet. It's all quiet."

She stood at ease before him, just as she had done on that very first day they'd met in the mountains. "Let's hope they reveal themselves soon." She looked at him briefly before moving her gaze to a spot behind him on the wall. "It would be good if we could put this all behind us and go home."

He chewed on his lip and looked at the floor. "Yes, Sergeant, it would. I expect you're looking forward to getting back to your regiment."

She thought of her Fifth Infantry base in Fort Bliss, Texas. It felt like a million miles away from where she was at that moment. "Yes, sir."

He cleared his throat. "I'm pleased to have you in my unit, Sergeant Hanson." He looked out the window, focusing his eyes on the expanse of green beyond. "I remember you telling me you were disappointed not to feel accepted as one of the team."

She realized she had been holding her breath. She let it out. "You remember me saying that?"

"Of course," he said. "From what I recall, you were pretty angry with me."

"I was."

He smiled. "And I can see why."

She allowed herself to look at him; he was studying her face.

"I want you to know that you are, and always will be, one of the team." He broke off for a moment. "Wherever you go and whatever you do, always remember that."

"Thank you, sir." She hoped he hadn't noticed the crack in her voice.

"I…wanted to say…" He closed his eyes.

"Say what?" she whispered.

But he clearly didn't hear her because he was back to formality. "I wanted to say that I'll write an excellent reference for you when I compile my report about this mission."

She bowed her head. "Thank you, sir."

He stood in silence. She watched his face struggle to contain whatever emotions were battling within him.

"I wish I'd met your father," he said. She almost lost her balance at the directness of the statement.

"My dad? Why would you have wanted to meet my dad?"

"Because you loved him," he said. "I suspect he's the first person you think of in the morning and last thing at night. He's the most important man in your life."

"It used to be that way," she said quietly, "but not anymore."

"I hope you can find a man even half as good as him," he said. "You deserve it."

She lowered her eyes, determined not to let him see her cry again. "Thank you, sir. I hope so, too."

She felt his stare remain on her face for a few seconds, but knew she couldn't allow herself to look at him. She couldn't risk meeting his eyes and opening herself to his perceptive scrutiny. He knew too much already.

He sensed her discomfort. "Major Moore is making breakfast. I'll relieve you of lookout duty when it's ready."

She nodded, unable to speak, willing him to leave quickly.

He turned around. She breathed out.

He turned back. "Sergeant Hanson, please remember what I said yesterday. Whatever happens, forget about me and keep yourself safe."

She nodded. It was all she could do.

He left the room. She returned to her post, resolving to ignore his advice, and she picked up from where she had left off.

Dean had no appetite for breakfast—he had no appetite for anything. His stomach was awash with emotions, and his chest was tight with pain. He couldn't bear being this close to Cara and not reaching out to touch her. It took all the discipline he had in his body. But it had to be this way. He couldn't afford to care about her more than he did already. It would weaken him and make him liable to sloppiness and mistakes. He must remain focused and sharp because it was the only way he would be able to fight alongside her as a soldier, and allow them to defeat the enemy together.

He'd come to the conclusion that he could stand by her side as a comrade in arms but not as someone more than that. In just six days, she had changed his entire view of women in combat, and he sensed he would never be the same again. He would never again make stereotyped assumptions about a female soldier's ability to do a job professionally and effectively. He would not assume that their lack of strength and physical size made them lesser soldiers on the battlefield. What Cara lacked in stature, she made up for in sheer determination and gutsiness.

He stirred his coffee slowly. She would make a man proud one day, just as she had made her father proud. He closed his eyes and said a silent prayer, asking God to take her into the arms of a man who would value her strengths and weaknesses alike, cherishing her vulnerability, and not using it against her.

Chris placed a plate of scrambled eggs in front of him. He pushed it away.

"Eat up," Chris encouraged. "You're no good to anyone on an empty stomach."

Dean stood up. "I told Sergeant Hanson that I'd relieve her of duty so she can eat. I'll go get her."

Chris put his hand on his friend's shoulder. "Dean, you okay?"

He nodded. "Sure, I'm fine."

"I'm sorry if I overstepped in the car," Chris said. "You know, about you and Sergeant Hanson. I should've just kept my mouth shut."

"It's not a problem," Dean said, shrugging his shoulders. "You were right. I have let myself get too close to her. It's time I pulled back and concentrated on the job at hand. I don't need any distractions right now."

Chris took his hand off Dean's shoulder. "So you're pulling up the shutters? Just blocking it all out?"

"I'm doing what needs to be done. I have a job to do and so does Sergeant Hanson. The battlefield requires a strong mind and commitment to serving your country. There's no place for emotion when you're facing the enemy." He shook his head. "I need to focus on doing my job and put her out of my mind."

"I'm sorry, buddy," Chris said. "I can see this is hard for you."

"Hard doesn't even come close," he replied. "But I'll get over it."

Chris lowered his voice. "Are you still sticking to the story that you aren't in love with her?"

"That's my official story," Dean said, raising a weak smile. "It could do untold damage to my reputation if I was found out. Tough men don't fall in love, right?"

Chris patted him on the back. "Your secret's safe with me." He looked his friend squarely in the eye. "If that's what you think is best."

"It is," Dean said. "She'll be home soon, God willing, and I can try and forget her."

"And what about what Cara wants, Dean? What if she doesn't want to go home? What if she wants to stay with you?"

"Cara doesn't want a man like me. She needs a man who'd step back and let her run free. She doesn't need a protector, she needs an equal partner."

"What's stopping *you* from being her equal partner?"

Dean stopped and searched his mind for the answer to that question. He thought of his mother and his sister.

"I can't change," he said, shaking his head. "I tried, and I prayed about it, and I really thought I could do it. But every time I see her, I want to stand in front of her and stop anything from getting through. She doesn't want a man like that."

"How do you know what she wants?" Chris challenged. "Have you asked her?"

"No," Dean said with force, "and I don't intend to ask her, either."

Chris raised his eyes to the ceiling. "How long have I known you?"

"A long time. Twelve years, maybe more."

Chris laughed. "I remember you being such a hotheaded young rookie. You wanted to save the whole world."

Dean chuckled at the memory. "Yeah, I've calmed down a bit since then."

"You still want to save the world, though, right?"

The smile faded on Dean's face. "Not the whole world, just a few people within it."

Chris pulled a chair from the table and straddled it, sitting close to his friend in the quiet of the kitchen. "In all the time I've known you, I've never seen you open up and let anyone in. This might be your one chance of happiness. Don't let it pass you by, because you'll regret it one day."

Dean clenched his fists. "I…can't."

Chris spoke softly. "Do you really think that God wants you to spend the rest of your life alone?"

Dean sighed. "I don't deserve any grace from God."

Chris slapped him gently on the back. "None of us do, buddy. You don't have to earn God's grace. It's free. Seems to me that Cara came into your life for a reason."

Dean said nothing for a while, bowing his head at the table. He imagined Cara sitting in a sunny garden beside a rose-covered house with a child at her feet. In his vision the door of the house opened, and a man stepped out onto the deck, smiling. He opened his eyes, realizing that the man in the vision was him. This scene was most definitely not part of the mission brief. It wasn't part of his plan at all. He pushed his chair back and stood up, shaking the image away.

"Cara will find someone special someday," he said. "Someone who can give her everything she needs."

Chris clicked his tongue in frustration. "So you just walk away?"

"I walk away," Dean said, turning to leave the kitchen. "She's better off without me."

His footsteps felt like lead as he headed upstairs to the

small room where he would find Cara Hanson, silently huddled beside the window, expertly searching the landscape for the danger that would soon visit them.

Cara yawned and looked at her watch: 7:00 p.m. The sun was teetering on the edge of the mountains, and her small room was bathed in a warm orange glow. She had walked through the cabin every hour, checking each side, finally coming upon something that had concerned her. She'd noticed a small, leafy shrub beyond the meadow on the edge of the woodland. It looked oddly out of place, sitting alone in scrubland, partially hidden by the dark trunk of a tree. She'd watched it carefully, magnifying its position as much as she could. As a sniper, her instincts usually never failed her. She was unsettled.

She found Dean sitting in the kitchen with an open Bible on the table in front of him. She stopped in the doorway, unwilling to disturb his private time of reflection. But, as always, he sensed her presence and turned around. He closed the book.

"What is it, Sergeant?" His voice was flat and emotionless. He had seemed to flip a switch since arriving back at the cabin, shutting her out completely.

"There's something you need to see, sir," she said, stretching out her hand and beckoning him to follow.

She took the lead and showed him the shrub through the window. He used her binoculars to study it carefully before handing them back to her.

"It's just a plant, Sergeant—a harmless bush."

She shook her head. "But I've never seen it there before."

"Maybe you missed it?"

She shook her head even harder. "I never miss anything," she said. "It wasn't there before. I'm sure of it."

He looked again at the small shrub sitting, quite benignly, blowing gently in the breeze.

"I'll go check it out."

"That's a bad idea," she said. "If someone is lying in wait, you'll be taken totally by surprise. That's what they want you to do."

"Okay, Sergeant, what would *you* do?"

"Let me shoot the ground right by it," she said. "If it's just a shrub, it'll stay exactly where it is. If it's something more sinister, chances are, it'll move pretty quickly."

"Just one bullet," he said. "We don't want to be wasting ammo on shooting the plant life outside."

"Just one bullet," she confirmed. "That's all I need."

He stood back as she crouched low by the window. She lined up her shot with perfect accuracy, deciding to focus on a small stone sitting just to the right of the oddly placed shrub. She brought her face slowly to the telescopic sight, and everything else melted away. She squeezed the trigger.

The stone shot into the air as it was hit with dead-on precision. No sooner had it landed back on the ground, than the shrub jumped to its feet and ran into the cover of the woods. She stood up, turned to Dean and raised her eyebrows. His face was a picture of amazement.

"That was exceptional work, Sergeant," he said, placing his hand on her shoulder before quickly snatching it away again and straightening up.

"I guess it's safe to say that we're being watched," she said. "We need to make a plan. Do we shoot to kill or take into custody?" She needed to know. She needed to prepare.

He continued to stand in wonder. She was pleased to see that he had recognized her skill of perception in identifying a shrub, among thousands, that wasn't part of the natural landscape. Her abilities had thwarted the danger for now, but she still needed to know how this would end.

He suddenly snapped back to attention. "Personally speaking, I'd like to see these guys spend the rest of their days in a military prison rather than taking the easy way out."

Cara nodded in agreement.

"But we need to hold a briefing session with Major Moore first," he said. He took one last glance out the window. "We take just five minutes out, discuss tactics and get back to work."

His manner was brusque and professional, and traces of the Dean she'd seen slowly emerge over the last six days had all but vanished. He'd locked her out of his heart, and she couldn't stop a pain spreading its way across her chest.

She followed him into the living room where Chris was standing, radio in hand with a look of shock on his face. He was breathing quickly and his pallor was waxy.

"Chris," Dean said, clearly concerned. "Is everything okay? We've got trouble, and we need to make a plan."

Chris looked directly at Cara. "Oh, we've got trouble, all right," he said forcefully.

Cara turned to face Dean, confused by the sudden change in Chris's manner towards her.

Dean sidestepped to be close to her side. "What's going on, Chris?"

Chris stepped toward them, eyeing Cara's gun suspiciously. She instinctively brought her hand to rest on the holster. She didn't pop it open but she was ready.

"We've just received a message from the IT technician at the Texas Department of Motor Vehicles. He's managed to access the plate record for the SUV," Chris said. His face looked to be set in stone. "It's registered to someone currently serving in the U.S. Army, someone close to Special Forces."

Cara's heart dropped into the pit of her stomach. She sensed something was terribly wrong. "Who is it?"

Chris came to stand directly in front of her. She saw his eyes flash with derision.

"It's *you*, Sergeant," he said. "The plate is registered to you."

TWELVE

Dean tensed as Cara jumped back. "No!" she gasped.

Chris's eyes never left hers. "I can assure you, Sergeant Hanson, it is true."

Dean remained by Cara's side. "Do you know anything about this?"

"No," she said, panic and confusion evident on her face. "I never saw that car before it tried to run us off the road in Wyoming. I promise you it has nothing to do with me."

"I think you know more than you're telling us, Sergeant," Chris said, walking to stand over her small frame. "Why would a car plate, used by known terrorists, turn out to be registered to a U.S. Military sniper?"

"They must've changed the state record in order to frame me," Cara said, looking into his eyes, pleading. "You, of all people, know what it feels like to be set up. They're trying to divide us."

Dean stepped between Chris and Cara, gently pushing his friend back. "Chris, listen to me, this doesn't make any sense. Sergeant Hanson has been with me for six days and I trust her implicitly. There's no doubt in my mind that she's been set up. We know someone hacked into the Texas vehicle-registration records. They've clearly planted this false information."

"You assume that's true," Chris said. He pointed a finger at Cara. "But I don't think we can trust her."

Dean tried hard to retain his composure. "You don't know her like I do, Chris. She wouldn't betray her country."

Chris kept his eyes trained on Cara's Glock in its holster as he spoke. "You're an exceptional soldier, Dean, but in this case, your judgment is too clouded to make an impartial assessment."

Dean folded his arms. "My judgment is not in question here. I know Sergeant Hanson far better than you, and I can vouch for her honesty."

Chris looked slowly between Cara and Dean. "You've been totally taken in by her act," he said. "I must admit, I was fooled by her, too, but I'm not in deep like you are. You'd do anything to protect her and say anything to save her."

Dean pulled himself up to his full height. "I'd do the same for you."

"I say we can't take any chances," Chris said. "We have to take her weapons away."

"No!" Cara said loudly. "Without a weapon, I'm useless."

"And without a weapon, she's totally exposed," Dean said. "I can't let you take her only means of defense away."

Chris began to pace the floor. "What about our defense, Dean?" He pointed to the window. "We're already facing an unknown enemy outside—we can't fight one on the inside, as well."

"We know the enemy is already here," Dean said, trying to refocus Chris's mind on the danger at their door.

Chris stopped pacing. "How?"

"Sergeant Hanson just identified a shooter, probably a sniper, camouflaged in the woods. I would never have spotted it, never in a million years. Whoever is out there is highly trained and clever at avoiding detection." He glanced at Cara. "We need her skills."

Chris ran a hand over his face, revealing the tiredness beneath his skin.

"I want to trust her the same way as you," Chris said, "but one of us has to remain objective. Emotional connections between soldiers put the whole team at risk. I care about you a whole lot, buddy, but I'd never lay down my weapon for you and leave myself wide open. She's got a hold over you that makes you weak." Chris's face took on a grave expression. "You said so yourself, she's made you vulnerable."

Dean's heart hammered in his chest. He couldn't deny the words coming from Chris's mouth. Cara *did* make him weak, she *did* make him vulnerable and she *did* put him at risk in so many different ways, not just as a soldier. He knew that he could never serve alongside her again. But he knew he could trust her. He knew the secrets of her heart.

He stepped forward and crossed his arms. "If you want to disarm Sergeant Hanson, you'll have to go through me first."

Chris punched his fist into the palm of his hand. "I knew you'd never turn your back on her. I know how strongly you feel." He shook his head. "But I'll be watching her like a hawk. If you're wrong about her, we're all in serious danger."

"I'm not wrong," Dean said. "She's the one who fought in your corner when you were out there all alone. She made me question everything I'd been told about you. She saw your true character when everyone else had you marked as a traitor."

Chris stopped in his tracks. His features briefly softened.

"I wish I could trust her, but I can't argue with the evidence. I can't let her suck me in like she's done with you."

"No," Cara said, stepping forward. "You've got me all wrong, Major. Let's discuss this calmly."

"I need to take lookout duty upstairs," he said, ignoring her request. "I've had enough of this cat-and-mouse game. When I spot something out there, I'm taking it down. We take no prisoners. We shoot to kill."

"Let Hanson take the shots," Dean said. "She's our best line of defense."

Chris narrowed his eyes. "I think I'll take my own shots," he said, turning and striding up the stairs.

Dean turned to Cara. "You okay?" he asked gently. "That must've been a pretty nasty surprise."

She looked shell-shocked. "It's a setup," she said quietly.

"Don't you think I know that?" he said. "There was never a doubt in my mind."

She brought her face up to meet his. "What did Major Moore mean when he said I make you weak? He said he knew how strongly you feel about me." She took a quick breath. "How *do* you feel about me?"

Dean bit his tongue inside his mouth and clenched his fists tight, pressing his nails into his palms.

"Major Moore has this wild idea that I'm in love with you," he said, mustering the best smile he could manage.

She blinked fast. "In love with me?" she repeated. "Why would he think that?"

"Because I want to look after you, keep you out of harm's way, all the things that drive you crazy."

"Is that all?"

"Yes, Sergeant, that's all."

She looked at the floor. "Major Moore has been through a stressful time. He's clearly not thinking straight."

Dean swallowed back the lump that had developed in his throat. "No, he's definitely on the wrong track with that stupid theory."

Her saw her take another quick breath. "Of course," she said. "It's a ridiculous idea."

He saw the way her shoulders dropped and a look of pain swept over her face. His stomach flipped. Did she look *disappointed?*

She composed herself. "I'm sorry, sir, for kissing you at the lake." She broke off and looked up. "I let my emotions overcome me. I hope you didn't read too much into it."

"No need to apologize, Sergeant," he said, remembering how soft and warm her lips felt and how he had been transported to a place of perfect tranquility. "Everybody lets their guard down sometimes."

"Even you?"

He stared into her eyes, unblinking. Her blue eyes had lost none of the intensity they'd shown at their first meeting and they now rested on his face, waiting for a response.

"No," he said, finally. "I can't afford to let my guard down. There's too much at stake."

She reached up to touch the cross that always hung from her neck. She gently smoothed it between her fingers. "Would you rather I wasn't here, sir?" she said.

"Yes," he said quickly, without thinking. He instantly tried to catch the word before it reached her ears. "I mean no. You're important to the team, Sergeant."

He closed his eyes, silently chastising himself for not considering his response more carefully. Of course he wished she wasn't there, facing a danger that he couldn't push back from their shores. He wished she was safe at home, far away from all this.

She nodded slowly. "It's okay," she said, although he suspected she didn't mean the words. "I understand."

"No," he said. "I don't think you do."

He watched her straighten her back and salute him.

"We have an important job to do, Captain," she said. "What are your orders?"

He wanted to go to her, wrap his arms around her, tell her how wonderful she was and how she made his heart leap. Instead, he breathed in deeply and said, "You take ground-floor lookout detail, Sergeant, while I assist Major Moore. Report any hostile forces immediately. With any luck, we'll all be home by the end of the day."

He turned to walk away. His feet felt heavy again, as if he was wading through treacle. He willed himself not to turn around and not to look in her face to see the expression of absolute betrayal that he felt sure was written upon it.

Cara set up her lookout post at the back door, overlooking the small porch, with excellent views into the trees and meadows. She had heard Dean and Major Moore upstairs continuing to discuss her allegiance to the team, with Dean defending her forcefully. She was grateful for Dean's loyalty to her, but she knew for certain now that his loyalty didn't extend anywhere near her expectations. He didn't want her there. She was still a woman in a man's world.

She shook her head. Why did this make her feel so empty inside? Why did her heart hurt in the same way it had done in the days and weeks after the death of her father? Thoughts of her father brought her mind back into sharp focus. Dean was still in danger and she was his best chance of survival. She decided not to judge him for his failings—he'd tried hard to accept her as a protector, but he couldn't let go of his past.

What about you? a little voice in her said. *Have you let go of your past?*

She shook the voice away and scanned the bushes and shrubs outside, searching for another unusual sight amongst the natural foliage. She couldn't forget the certainty of Chris's belief that she made Dean weak and vulnerable. And now Dean had confirmed this was true. He didn't want her there; he didn't want to be the one looking out for her, shielding her from harm. He was so focused on her that he was putting his own safety on the line.

In a flash, an idea hit her like a blow to the stomach. *She* was his weakest link. If she weren't there, he would be stronger and more capable.

She picked up her rifle and slotted it into her carry case. She would be able to flit, unseen, into the woods and set up a sniper position that would protect him from afar. If she could see for miles around, she would be able to take down any danger as it approached, preventing it from even reaching his door.

She gathered her ammunition before clicking open the back door to creep slowly, on all fours, onto the wooden porch. The swing chair creaked rhythmically by her side. She used it for cover while she assessed the movement of the tall grass in the meadow. Moving like a ghost in the night, she was gone in a second.

"She's gone," Dean called to Chris. "Cara's gone."

"I told you we couldn't trust her," Chris said, walking into the kitchen, as if this affirmed everything he'd already known.

Dean felt panic begin to tingle in his feet and travel through his body like fire.

"She's gone because she feels like she's dragging us down," he said. "She thinks we don't trust her to protect us."

"Let her go, Dean," Chris said.

"I can't let her go!" Dean shouted. He was surprised at the force of his own voice. "How can I carry on, knowing that she's out there, alone and exposed?"

Chris threw his hands in the air. "She's a trained sniper, Dean. She's more dangerous than you could ever imagine."

Chris's radio crackled on the window ledge, sending a low hiss through the tense air. The major picked it up and took it to the corner of the kitchen. Dean crouched low to the window at the door and searched the terrain outside, knowing it was futile to even try to find her. She was too good for that.

Chris appeared at his side, bending to squat next to him. His face was ashen.

"Dean," he said, putting his hand on his friend's shoulder. "I've just received a radio message from the Texas Department of Motor Vehicles." He hung his head. "You were right. The information regarding Cara's ownership of the plate was false. Just a few minutes ago the record was changed again to identify *you* as the owner. Someone's toying with us, and I walked right into their trap. I'm sorry."

Dean clenched his teeth. "It's a little late for apologies."

Chris closed his eyes and took a moment before speaking. "The hacker is apparently using complex military-coding techniques to bypass security systems. It's beyond the expertise of the Texas police. I wish I'd known this information before I assumed Sergeant Hanson was guilty."

Dean stood up. "Have you got any idea what you've done?" he said angrily, looking down at Chris. "You accused her of being a traitor and now she's gone."

Chris put his head in his hands. "I'm so sorry, Dean. I've been alone for too long, not knowing who to trust. It's made me edgy, and I messed up."

Dean walked purposefully to the radio resting on the

window ledge. "I'm calling in the Nineteenth Airborne Group. Gantry said they'd be on standby. With Cara gone and your mind playing tricks on you, we're in no shape to fight a guerrilla war. Reinforcements can be here in an hour and scour every inch of the area to find whoever is out there."

"I know you're angry, Dean, but if you call more troops here, the terrorists will just vanish again. This is our best chance of bringing them down."

Dean walked to the wall and raised his hand, landing a heavy punch to the papered plasterboard. "But Cara is out there alone," he said, feeling a satisfying throb begin to pulsate in his knuckles. "Anything could happen to her. She's on her own."

Chris laced his fingers together and wrapped them tight around the back of his neck.

"She's not entirely on her own," he said.

"Of course she's on her own," Dean said, allowing his voice to rise again. "There's no one else here."

Chris stood up and nodded his head toward the kitchen counter where the black, leather-bound Bible had been sitting since their arrival at the cabin. The space was empty.

Cara settled into the prone position, adjusting the leaves around her body. She had gathered a wide selection of shrubs and plants, choosing those with the densest coverage. She'd worked quickly, weaving the branches into a shield, providing her with a cloak of invisibility. It would enable her to move through the long grass, undetected, sneaking up on her prey and disabling them before they could get anywhere near the cabin. Dean would, hopefully, never even need to draw his weapon.

She waited patiently in the warmth of the setting sun, knowing that it was only a matter of time before the enemy sniper returned. She was right. A flock of birds flew into the air and she watched them scatter in the sky, amid much squawking and beating of wings.

She smiled. "I see you," she whispered.

The sniper was well hidden amongst the trees of the woodland, about a half mile away, and it was difficult to trace a perfect line of sight through the heavy trunks. She could certainly hit him from this angle but it would give away her position, and she wasn't sure how many others were in the vicinity. She knew he was unlikely to be working alone. He was probably waiting for the enemy to be lured out into the open, to leisurely pick them off one by one. This was an organized attack. They might have seen her leaving the cabin, but she felt certain she'd hidden herself from sight with her slow movements through the grass.

She licked her lips and crawled slowly back on her belly to give herself a better view of the sniper's position and to assess his aim. Where was he intending to fire?

Everything was so quiet and so calm that what happened next almost felt like a dream.

She caught sight of a soldier emerging from under cover of the trees. He was wearing a full ghillie suit, walking steadily through the woods toward the cabin. She took a second to register his intentions and gasped as she realized that on his shoulder rested the long black barrel of an M72 rocket launcher. And he was aiming straight at the cabin.

The soldier continued his path to his destination, and she knew it was now or never. Neither Dean nor Chris would spot him in time to stop his attack. She wanted the head shot, to take him down without question, but his head was obscured by the barrel of the launcher. She'd have to take the chest. She muttered her words of prayer and took him down. He crumpled to the floor, falling face front onto the grass. But he was still moving, still able to carry out his deadly intention.

"No!" she called, as the missile left his launcher and slammed into the side of the cabin, sending a deafening roar whooshing past her ears. The cabin tore apart like it was made of paper, and pieces of wood flew through the air, mixed with fire, smoke and the debris of her entire life.

The breath was sucked from her body. She almost stood up and started running wildly to the gaping hole that had appeared in the cabin's side wall, shouting for Dean, desperate to know he was still alive. But she didn't. Her training kicked in and she lined up the solider on the ground in her sights once again. She took him out with a shot that she was absolutely sure neutralized the threat beyond all doubt. She then turned to the sniper in the woods. He was gone!

Without any care for her own life, she then rose from her position of safety and raced to the cabin, feeling sickness rising in her stomach. Only when she reached the wreckage site did she realize that she'd left her rifle nestled in the long grass. A shot ringing out from the woods let her know that it was too late to retrieve it. The enemy sniper was making his attack.

She scrambled over the rubble of the cabin, toward the hole where the remains of her living room were clearly visible. She saw the body of a man sprawled on the stairs. His clothes were black and charred, but he was coughing, and he was alive. She dropped to her knees and turned him over to see the charcoal-smeared face of Major Moore.

"Dean," Chris sputtered. "Go find Dean."

She stood up, breathing hard as her eyes darted back and forth amid the wreckage. She couldn't see him. She started to panic. She closed her eyes and prayed. Then she began searching. In a corner of the living room where the damage was less severe, she thought she saw movement. She weaved her way to the corner, her heart leaping like never before when Dean's face came into view. But he was in pain, his left arm and leg pinned down by a heavy, solid-wood bookcase.

"Cara," he called, showing his relief at seeing her. "You're okay."

She dropped to his side and touched his face. "I'm okay," she said. "But there's a sniper out there. We need to get you on your feet." She grabbed the bookcase and pulled with all her might. "It…won't…move," she said breathlessly.

Dean reached up and seized her hand, squeezing it tightly. "Cara, get out of here," he said, looking into her eyes. "Please, get yourself away from danger."

"I won't leave you," she said, stroking his hair.

"You must," he pleaded, looking down at his body, pinned against the floor. "I can't protect you like this."

"Then let *me* protect *you*," she said, pulling an upturned table across the floor to act as a makeshift barrier. "Whatever happens, I won't leave your side."

"No, Cara," he protested. "You have a chance to save yourself. Don't sacrifice your life for me. I'm not worth it."

She lay by his side and put her hand on his cheek, resting her eyes on his. "I know I'd rather die by your side than spend the rest of my life without you."

Dean knew that he was powerless—powerless to lift the bookcase that had smashed down on him in the blast and powerless to send Cara away from his side. He watched her dragging items across the floor to build a strong defense around him, before returning to help Chris move behind the barrier. The major sat heavily on the floor, holding his right arm tightly across his chest.

"It's broken," he said. "I guess I'll have to shoot with my left hand."

Dean gripped Cara's hand. "I called in the Nineteenth Airborne Group an hour ago. They'll be here soon. You could slip away into the woods unseen." Dean looked over at Chris, silently conveying his thoughts. "Major Moore and I can hold the fort here while you go search for the sniper outside."

Cara was loading bullets into her handgun. She stopped and turned to Dean. "I meant what I said. I'm not leaving your side. You and Major Moore are seriously incapacitated. You don't stand a chance of survival without me."

"She's right, Dean," Chris said, cradling his oddly twisted arm by his side. He gave a small, hollow laugh. "Imagine what the guys at the base would think if they could see us now, both holed up in a corner being protected by a woman."

"They'd think you were incredibly fortunate," Cara said, smiling through the tension.

Chris tried to stand, but his legs buckled beneath him and he sank to the floor. "I'd like to take this opportunity to say sorry to you, Sergeant Hanson. I should never have doubted you and caused you to leave."

"No need to apologize," said Cara. "If I'd stayed at my lookout post here, I'd be dead by now."

Chris turned his head to the place where Cara had set up her post, a place that had been torn apart, revealing the sinews of the building beneath. "Someone is watching over you, Sergeant," he said.

"Someone is watching over all of us," she said, catching Dean's eyes in hers.

He smiled at her, feeling his pain being replaced with a warm glow. He'd never felt so close to her as he did at that moment, despite his feelings of desperation regarding her safety. This was a new experience for him and he felt humbled by it. *He* was usually the protector—*he* was the one who confronted danger, and *he* was the one who shepherded the vulnerable to safety. Now he knew how it felt to be in the others' shoes.

Cara crawled to his side as if she'd been able to read his mind. "Whatever happens," she whispered in his ear, "I want you to know I've been incredibly proud to serve alongside you."

He felt his heart soaring to hear these words of praise and comfort fall from her mouth. He had never dared believe that she might think of him as more than a commanding officer.

Dean felt undeserving of such praise from a soldier he had almost sent back to base. It was *he* who should feel proud to serve alongside *her*. "I'm sorry, Cara," he said. "I wanted you to leave because I couldn't bear to see you hurt." He gritted his teeth as the pain returned. "It's not because you're a woman. It's because you mean so much more to me than a soldier. Losing a soldier is hard but losing you would be more than I can take."

He reached for her hand and she took it. Her fingers were smooth and warm on his battle-scarred skin.

"You won't lose me," she whispered into his ear. "Just trust that this is all meant to be. Let it go."

She moved her mouth from his ear, brushing against his cheek and resting her lips on his. The crushing weight pressing down on his chest vanished in an instant and he was soaring high, floating on clouds.

"Hanson!" Major Moore's voice was loud and urgent, shattering their perfect moment.

Cara sprang to her feet, pulling her Glock into the air. Dean couldn't see what was happening but he heard Cara firing rapidly. Enemy fire was returned in equal measure.

His own weapon had been blown from his grasp and too badly damaged to fire. Chris was attempting to provide backup support, but his left arm action looked to be wild and ineffective. Dean found himself totally reliant upon Cara to keep the danger at bay. How much longer could she hold out?

His ears caught the sound of helicopter blades whirring in the distance. Help was at hand. He almost let himself believe that they would make it out together—almost!

Cara's pistol clicked as she pulled the trigger. She clicked again.

"I'm out," she shouted, turning to look at Chris on the floor, gritting his teeth through his pain.

"Me, too," he said.

Cara began to search frantically in her bag for more bullets. Dean watched her pulling out empty boxes, muttering, "No, no, I won't let this happen again."

He extended his hand and managed to catch her arm, pulling her down to his side.

"Now is your chance, Cara," he said. "Go."

She seemed to calm under his touch and her breathing became shallow. She lay her body down next to his and put her head on his shoulder.

"Never," she whispered. "I'll never go."

Dean couldn't stop the tears from rolling down his face as he buried his face in Cara's soft hair. This wasn't how the story was supposed to end. He was supposed to save her.

Bullets from the sniper continued to rain down on them. He was coming closer, gaining more accuracy every second. Dean tried to turn his body to shield Cara from the inevitable bullet but his body was too tightly pinned. He tried to push Cara away instead, but she realized what was happening and clung to him even tighter, using the entire length of her tiny frame to cover as much of his body as possible.

He never even heard the bullet hit; he never heard her scream. But he felt the warm blood as it oozed from her stomach and onto his skin. He held her close in his arms as her face changed to one of serenity and peace, blinking slowly until her eyes closed completely.

THIRTEEN

Dean kept vigil by Cara's bedside, cradling her cold hands in his, praying more fervently than he ever had. Machines beeped and whirred in the silence of her small hospital room, artificially sustaining her fragile existence. He had refused medical treatment himself, insisting on staying by her side at all times, standing guard outside the operating room where she had undergone life-saving surgery on a perforated stomach. The bullet had traveled through her back and lodged in her rib cage, containing the danger within her own body and preventing it from traveling into his. No sooner had she been hit than the Nineteenth Airborne Group dropped from the sky, engaging the enemy in a fierce gun battle. Two rebel soldiers had later been found fatally wounded, but a third had made his escape. The danger hadn't been totally eliminated. Someone was still out there, possibly watching and waiting to finish the job he started.

Dean choked on a sob as he brushed Cara's cheek, still beautiful and smooth in spite of her devastating internal injuries. She had been willing to give up her life to save his, and he knew that she would not regret a single moment of it. He knew with certainty that he would never be able to change her, and he finally realized that he wouldn't want to.

It was as though the scales had fallen from his eyes. His desire to protect her and save her from harm was his own reflection of her. She had smashed this image and redrawn it, using her own hand to complete the picture.

He looked at her small, wounded body and saw a woman who would stand up and be counted, refuse to be led astray and never allow her moral compass to deviate from the right path.

The door opened, and Major Moore stepped into the room. He wore a large white cast on his right arm.

"How's she doing?" he asked gently, putting his hand on Dean's arm.

"She's a fighter. The doctor said the next twenty-four hours are the crucial ones."

Chris rubbed Dean's shoulder. "She'll pull through. This world needs women like Cara Hanson." He tried to laugh but it came out hard and awkward.

Dean wished that Chris would leave. He needed time alone to silence the voice in his head—the one telling him that Cara might die—because she'd saved him.

Please God, he prayed, *don't send her into my life only to take her away again.*

"I brought you this," Chris said, reaching down and putting a familiar black Bible on the crisp white sheets. "I found it in Cara's bag."

Dean picked up the Bible and held it close to his chest, feeling a small seed of comfort being sowed within. In this depth of despair, God was his only hope and he decided to take refuge in His eternal promise. He opened the page at Cara's bookmark. It was Psalm 121: *I will lift up my eyes to the mountains; from where shall my help come?* He smiled, wondering if this had guided her in her time of need, or if it was guiding her now, showing her the way home.

"We're really blessed she was there," Chris said, breaking through his thoughts. "She bought us just enough time."

Dean nodded, reminding himself that she had taken the bullet meant for him.

"The two bodies recovered from the cabin have been identified," Chris said quietly, clearly uncertain of whether this was an appropriate time to speak of it.

"Who are they?" Dean asked, unable to stop his anger from bursting forth.

"Two former corporals from the Ninety-Fifth Field Artillery Regiment. They were dishonorably discharged from the army two years ago after a tour of Afghanistan, where they distributed anti-U.S. propaganda." Chris went to stand at the foot of the bed in the dimly lit room. Outside, it was dark and raining, echoing a soft patter through the air. "A stockpile of weapons has been recovered from their homes. At least they can't hurt anyone else now."

Dean looked up. "But they're not from Special Forces, are they?" he said, rubbing the smooth metal rail with his hands. "Our traitor is still out there."

"I've asked Gantry to pull the photo records of all serving Special Forces Personnel in Tenth Group," Chris said. "I may be able to spot a familiar face among them. I won't rest until I find who's at the top of this organization. Their SUV is being forensically analyzed, as well. The net is closing in on these guys, Dean. Just wait and see."

"Has there been any more news from the Texas Department of Motor Vehicles?"

Chris grimaced. "They haven't managed to crack the hacker's code, but Gantry's put a team of military experts on it. It won't be long now."

Dean smiled at Chris to let him know that he didn't blame his friend for his error of judgment about Cara—it had likely saved her from being killed by the blast in the first place. The major's distrust had turned out to be her good fortune.

"Gantry has posted a guard at the door," Chris continued. "If there is another threat heading this way, it won't get through to hurt her again." He dropped his voice. "Sheila Hanson has been informed. She's on her way from Hurricane."

Dean banged his forehead on his knuckles, gripping the rail. Sheila Hanson! How could he ever look her in the eye, knowing that Cara was fighting for her life because his had been spared?

"Dean, you look exhausted," Chris said. "You've been sitting here for six hours. I'll go grab you a cup of coffee and something to eat."

Dean forced a smile. The last thing he wanted to do was eat but he knew Chris needed to feel like he was helping.

"Sure," he said. "Thanks."

Chris slapped Dean lightly on the back and left the room, leaving him to resume his vigil by the bedside of the woman whose life he would gladly exchange for his own.

Cara found herself walking through woodland, feeling the warmth of the sun on her face. It was a beautiful summer's day and she knew this place well. She'd walked the same path hundreds of times before, heading for the stunning turquoise waters of Bear Lake. She felt at peace, knowing she was safe, surrounded by the natural world in which she was raised. It didn't seem unusual for her not to have her rifle. Somehow she knew that this world didn't need guns.

She crested the brow of a hill to see a scene below that had been playing in her head for as long as she could remember. In the distance, she saw her father at the banks of the lake, crouched low, watching the majestic deer. She automatically turned her head quickly, expecting to see the hunter emerging from the trees. But he wasn't there. Instead, she simply saw the rhythmic swaying of the branches and heard the uplifting song of birds. This was a different scene. She didn't feel afraid or panicked—she felt serene.

Her father rose to his feet and waved at her, calling her name. She began to run to him, reaching his side in just a fraction of the time it ought to have taken. She put her arms around his neck, and he drew her close, kissing her cheek. She pulled away and ran her hand over his shirt—the shirt that was awash with blood the last time she had seen him.

"There are no broken hearts here," he said, lifting her chin to his face. She saw that his face was just the same as it always was, with a gray-flecked beard running wildly across his chin and cheeks.

"I'm sorry, Dad," she said. "I'm sorry I didn't save you."

He smiled. "Oh, but you did, Cara," he said. "You did save me, every day of my life."

"No," she said, shaking her head. "I saw you die."

He took her hand and put it to his chest, to the place where the bullet had pierced him and taken him from her. She felt his heart beating beneath the fabric, strong and steady.

"You saw me leave," he said. "It was my time."

She smiled and pulled him close, remembering how sturdy and secure his arms had felt to her as a child.

"Let's go home, Dad," she said, linking his arm through hers and turning toward the hill, back to the cabin that they both loved so much.

He pulled her back. "No, Cara. I can't go with you. You'll have to find the way back yourself."

She looked up to the hill, realizing that the path had grown a thick layer of brambles and thorns in the short time she had left it.

"But I can't do it by myself," she said, dragging his arm to follow her. "It's too hard."

He smiled. "Lift your eyes to the mountains," he said, pointing to a figure standing tall and erect at the top of the hill. "Someone is waiting for you. He'll help you through."

She faced her father, holding his hands in hers. "You really can't come?"

"No, sweetheart. I'll wait for you here. I'll always be waiting here."

He kissed her hand and let it go. She then turned around and started to pull back the brambles, creating a path back to the top of the hill where she knew the cabin would be visible through the woods. The tall, dark figure was still waiting at the brow and she squinted against the sun, trying to make out the features of his face. Sunlight streamed onto his profile, highlighting the square jaw and crooked bridge of the nose. It was Dean! He had come for her, and her heart rose with joy.

She breathed hard as it dawned on her just how far away he was and how difficult it would be to reach him. She didn't know if she had the strength to carry on. She looked behind to see her father standing by the blue waters of Bear Lake, urging her to go forward, not back. She concentrated on every footstep, steadily taking them one by one. She heard Dean calling her name. He looked so distant, yet his voice was so close.

Suddenly, a pulsating pain in her stomach began to throb, and she remembered a bullet slamming into her back, sending red-hot fire slicing through her abdomen. She gritted her teeth against the pain and carried on walking, tearing at the brambles with her bare hands, desperately trying to open a pathway to Dean. She couldn't figure out how she could hear his words and feel his breath on her face, but she knew he was near, despite being so far away. His voice was clear and smooth, softly whispering, *"I love you."*

It was all she needed to swallow back the hurt of the past and fight with all her heart, to fight her way to the man who was calling her home. She never looked back again.

Dean thought that he saw Cara's fingers twitch in his as he whispered into her ear, telling her to fight, telling her to come home to him, telling her that he loved her. He hadn't known how much he needed her until he'd met her, and he knew that he could never go back to his life before that moment. He had never believed that any woman could change him as she had done. He'd railed against her influence and forced her to fight him every step of the way, but she'd never given up on him. She could have abandoned him to his stubborn loneliness, yet she stayed, showing him the true strength of a woman. And now he couldn't imagine life without her.

He brushed her hand, telling her again to come back to him. He brought his mouth to her ear, speaking low and soft. The only woman he had ever professed love for was his mother, but this was totally different, and he prayed that Cara would have the chance to meet Diane McGovern one day—two women, different lives, but both leaving an imprint on him forever.

"Well, this is a touching little scene, isn't it?"

His head sprang up from where it had been bent over the bed. The voice behind him was sneering, dripping with venom. And it was very familiar. Dean jumped to his feet, reaching for his gun in its holster. No! He hadn't replaced his damaged and useless weapon, leaving him totally exposed. He'd been so focused on maintaining his bedside vigil that his usual careful attention to detail had deserted him. He'd failed to adhere to his most basic military training, and now he would be forced to defend Cara without a weapon. Turning to face his assailant, he found himself staggering backward in disbelief, grabbing the rail to hold himself up.

"No!" he gasped. "You're dead. Gomez saw you die."

Sergeant Hicks curled his mouth in a satisfied, mocking smile. "What would Sergeant Gomez know?" he said, spitting his words. "He was too busy looking at that pretty little sniper to notice anything else. Someone died, yes, but it wasn't me."

Dean looked behind Hicks to the half-open door where the soldier on duty was lying, spread-eagle on the white, tiled floor. It was just him and Hicks in the small hospital room. And Hicks held a powerful, fully automatic pistol by his side. The white bandage on his left wrist told him that this was the man who'd attacked Cara on her way back from Hurricane.

Hicks pointed his gun directly at Dean's chest. "Drag the guard in here. And don't even think about calling for help."

Dean mentally ran through his options: the only safe one was to obey the order. He walked to the guard, grabbed him by his collar and slid him across the floor into the room. The guy was breathing, but his hair was glistening with blood seeping from a gash behind his ear. Dean momentarily considered grabbing the guard's gun from its holster. No, it was too risky. Cara's life depended on him handling this situation delicately.

He stood up to face the sergeant whose "death" had

affected him deeply. "You betrayed your unit," he said. "You let us think we'd lost a man."

Hicks waved his weapon through the air erratically. "One of our other men died, blown apart by the explosion." He spun around, angrily. "Now, I hear we've lost two more men. Someone has to pay for their lives. I can't let them go unpunished."

Dean narrowed his eyes, watching Hicks pace the floor, holding tight to the pistol he was brandishing wildly.

"It's Moore I want," Hicks said. "He's a traitor to the UFA. He infiltrated our ranks, lied to us and tried to destroy us. Our group's code demands that I take revenge. If you keep quiet and don't make trouble, I'll let you and the sniper live. Don't try to be a hero, Captain."

Dean's mind raced. Why hadn't he asked Chris to leave his weapon in the room? He was now the only barrier between Cara and another bullet. And he was defenseless. He needed to keep Hicks talking, to give himself more time to think.

"You were a good soldier, Sergeant Hicks," Dean said. "Why did you throw it all away on an organization that hates the country you served?"

"The United Free Army does not hate America." Hicks spat every word. "We love America. That's why we take action to stop the government from dragging us into wars that just create more body bags."

"And you think that the best way to do it is to kill your comrades?"

Hicks looked at Dean, wide-eyed. "It got your attention, didn't it? After the bomb at Fort Bragg, suddenly everyone in the military knows who we are and started listening to our demands."

"You were the inside man at Fort Bragg, weren't you?" Dean said, shaking his head at the disappointment creeping into his heart. "I thought you were a decent man, Hicks." He looked at Cara lying in her bed. "Sergeant Hanson prayed for you."

Hicks laughed. "What good does praying ever do, huh? Didn't save those four soldiers at Fort Bragg, did it? This is a war, Captain, and in a war there will be casualties."

"Major Moore almost found you out," Dean said. "That's why you framed him."

A slow smile crept over Hicks's face. "The UFA protects its members well. We use codenames and our identities are always hidden, even from each other. But I found out that our newest recruit was doing a lot of digging, asking a lot of questions. So I did a bit of digging of my own." He tapped the side of his nose. "I stayed one step ahead of you. As soon as I found out Special Forces had planted a mole, it was easy to set him up. You're all so predictable." He laughed again. "I really enjoyed watching you chasing your tails, trying to take him out. All I had to do was sit back and watch you do the work for me."

"But it failed, didn't it, Hicks? Moore is still alive."

"Not for long," Hicks mocked, settling himself behind the door to lie in wait. "Remember, Captain, if you try and warn Moore, I'll take you down instantly." He jerked his head toward Cara. "That goes for the sniper, too."

"Okay, I understand." Dean held up his hands, knowing that Hicks was likely to put a bullet in him anyway once he'd dispensed with Chris. He suspected that the sergeant was reluctant to fire his weapon now for fear of alerting others to the sound. If Dean didn't act quickly, both he and Chris were dead men. That would leave Cara alone with a deranged and dangerous man.

A plan pinged in his head.

"You know, Hicks," he said in a voice as calm and friendly as he could manage, "what you said just then makes a lot of sense. The military has gone soft lately. It's not like it used to be."

Hicks narrowed his eyes at his former captain, assessing his motives. Finally, he seemed to accept the words as sincere. "I know what you mean." He gesticulated to Cara. "Once you start allowing women on the front line, men don't behave like men anymore. We should get back to how it used to be when men looked after their wives and daughters rather than fighting alongside them."

Dean nodded. "I agree, Sergeant. Truth is, I've always had a secret respect for the UFA. I just couldn't admit it." His heart thumped in his chest, certain that Hicks would see through his lies. But he didn't.

Hicks tilted his head. "You're just the kind of man we need in the UFA, Captain—tough, angry, ruthless. You could make a real difference if you joined us."

Dean turned away, pretending to struggle with the offer. "I'm not sure. There's a lot to think about."

Hicks stepped out from behind the door. "You'd be our highest-serving soldier and, if you prove yourself, you'd take overall command of our organization." His face took on a reverent expression, tantalized by the thought of such a high-ranking officer in their midst. "It's a great honor to be our leader."

Dean took a step toward Hicks and reached out to place a hand on his shoulder. "Indeed, it would be an honor," he said, feeling certain that he'd gained the confidence of the turncoat sergeant.

The patter of footsteps running in the corridor reached his ears. He spoke louder to cover the sound. "I'd be very interested to set up a meeting with your comrades and discuss this in more detail."

Behind Hicks's back, the door burst open, and Chris stood in the doorway, weapon drawn, ready to take a shot.

Dean's hand, resting on Hicks's shoulder, swiftly moved to his neck and a viselike grip was applied. The suddenness of the action took Hicks by surprise, and his eyes bulged in shock as the compression on his windpipe increased. He tried to raise his weapon but Chris sprang forward to disarm him. Hicks fell to his knees, his face slowly turning a deep shade of purple.

Chris put his hand on his friend's arm. "Dean, he's had enough. Let me take it from here."

Dean maintained his grip for another second or two. This man had been responsible for so much hatred and division in the family of U.S. forces that he wanted him to pay the ultimate price for his actions. Then he remembered Cara lying in the bed behind him, and he released his hand, sending Hicks crashing to the ground, coughing and spluttering. Chris produced a pair of cuffs from his pocket and secured them tightly in place.

"Gantry's men managed to decrypt the registration record of the SUV," Chris said, hauling the disgraced sergeant to his feet. "As soon as they said Hicks's name, I figured his death was a setup. There's no better cover than being dead, right?"

"Enjoy the victory while you can, guys," Hicks said between gasps. "Your time will come."

Moore dragged him to the door. "You'll have plenty of time to plan your attack from a cell in military jail."

Hicks kicked out and looked Dean squarely in the eye. "I should've known you were a sissy, McGovern. No real man would sit at a woman's bedside and cry."

Dean bored his eyes into Hicks's. "If you're a real man, Hicks, then God help us all."

"I'll take him to Gantry," Chris said. "You stay here with Cara. She needs you more than we do right now."

Dean looked over at the unconscious guard slumped

in the corner. "Get someone to come with a gurney for this guy, okay?"

Then he turned his attention back to Cara. He felt her close. He knew she was fighting hard, but she couldn't do it alone. He felt his lost faith returning to him in far greater strength than before. He knew that prayer wasn't just lip service to God—it had real power and impact. And in this battle, it was his only weapon.

As Hicks's shouts of protest faded in the corridor, Dean settled himself in the chair by her bed and resumed the fight.

Cara neared the brow of the hill, but the pain in her belly caused her to stumble. She reached out her arms to lessen the fall and felt herself being caught and lifted back to her feet. She looked up to see Dean's face smiling down at her, and she allowed her body to go limp in his arms.

She looked through the woods to the spot where the cabin had lain for decades, but it was a vacant void. As she gazed at the scenery she saw that the landscape was changing, falling away to leave just empty white space.

"I'm tired," she whispered. "I can't carry on."

"It's over," he whispered back. "You made it. All you have to do is open your eyes."

She wanted to let the blanket of tiredness envelop her and sleep in his arms, but he kept shaking her awake.

"Open your eyes, Cara," he said. "Open your eyes."

She blinked slowly, forcing her lids apart, feeling them sticky and tender like she was using them for the first time. She saw a white ceiling with harsh strip lighting and felt starched cotton sheets beneath her arms. She heard Dean's voice gently saying her name. Turning her head to the side, she saw him watching her, beaming widely and stroking the fingers of her right hand.

"Welcome back," he said, pulling her hand up to his lips and letting it brush his skin.

"You came for me," she croaked. Her throat was dry and scratchy. "I had the most incredible dream, and you were there, calling my name."

"I've been praying for you," he said. "I figured you needed a little help."

She squeezed his hand, wincing with pain as she moved her legs, remembering the injury that had led her to the hospital bed in the first place. She looked at Dean, surprised that her first thought had not been the level of injury he had sustained. She recalled the decimated cabin and the makeshift defenses she'd erected in the corner, but she didn't feel the familiar sense of panic rise in her throat, thinking of what harm might have come to him. She felt calm and peaceful, knowing that she was not infallible. She couldn't save everyone. She could only do her best and accept that pitfalls are part of life. She didn't fear failure any longer. There was only one thing she feared at that moment, and that was Dean leaving her side.

"Were you here the whole time?" she asked, uncertain whether she had heard Dean's distant voice correctly—the one whispering *"I love you."*

"I've been here ever since you were brought in, right by your side."

"Were you talking to me?"

"Yes."

"I heard a voice." Her breathing began to strain a little.

Dean leaned over the bed. "Don't try to talk. Just concentrate on getting strong again."

She pushed his hand away. "No," she said. "I have to know something."

He sat back and laughed softly as a smile crept over his

face. "Even when your body is weak, your mind is still as stubborn as an ox."

"The voice was telling me things, things that pushed me on, things that kept me going and…" She stopped.

"And what?" he urged.

"Things that made me happy," she said, looking at him sideways, trying to gauge his reaction. He continued to hold her hand in his, stroking her fingers. His face looked softer than she'd ever seen, with an expression of hope that mirrored her own.

He broke into a wide smile, his eyes crinkling at the corners. "Which one of us is going to say it first?" he said. "The suspense is killing me."

"You know me," she said, smiling through her physical pain. "I'm too obstinate to back down."

He pulled his chair closer to the bed, as close as he was able, and brought his face near hers. She knew his scent. It was as familiar as the air she breathed.

"I love you," he whispered.

She closed her eyes and thought of how far she'd come to reach this point. The road had been so hard to travel, impossible at times, but with God's help, she had trodden the path without doubt or complaint, accepting that her future was one which had been mapped out for her. She had never imagined that such a blessing would be bestowed upon her, and her heart wanted to burst with joy. She opened her eyes.

"I love you, too," she said, feeling the warmth of a tear trickle down the side of her face. He gently wiped it away with his hand. She felt the rough, calloused skin on her cheek and was reminded of their mission in the mountains, the first event that would trigger a series of others, as they saved each other from danger, stepping up when the other was too weak.

He seemed to know what she was thinking. "We make a good team," he said. "Together, nothing can defeat us."

"Partners," she said.

He looked deep into her eyes. "Partners for life."

EPILOGUE

Dean stood at the altar, anxiously awaiting the arrival of his bride. His best man, Major Christopher Moore, stood by his side, occasionally nudging his arm and reassuring him that it's the bride's prerogative to be late.

Dean turned to scan the congregation of the small Church in El Paso that he and Cara had joined since settling in the town. They chose a beautiful house in a leafy suburb, perfect for her to continue working at Fort Bliss. He had successfully transferred there himself, cementing their future together in the Southwest. He had never been happier.

Colonel Gantry was by far the most noticeable among those gathered there, standing head and shoulders above the rest in the front row with Dean's mom and sister. Diane McGovern waved at her son, handkerchief at the ready. The proud look on her face said it all, and he smiled at her, thankful that she had felt emotionally strong enough to travel, by herself, to be here on this day, the most important of his life.

Sheila Hanson approached him with a serene look on her face. In a matching suit and hat of powder-blue, she looked as regal as a queen.

"Don't look so worried, Dean," she said, "Cara's just keeping you on your toes by being fashionably late."

Dean took Sheila's hand and kissed her cheek. "I don't care if she's two hours late." He laughed. "As long as she says yes, that's all I care about."

Sheila squeezed his hand in reply. "Welcome to the family, Dean. I'm so pleased to be gaining you as a son."

Gomez appeared behind her shoulder, looking as though he'd taken considerable trouble to dress up for the occasion. "Aw, Sheila," he said in his typical teasing style, "I thought I was the only son-in-law you really wanted."

Sheila Hanson giggled like a teenager. "If I was twenty years younger, I'd marry you myself."

Gomez gave a deep belly laugh and took her hand. "Let's go sit down. Cara will be here any minute."

"One more thing, Sergeant," Dean said, shaking hands with Gomez. "How's the leg?"

Gomez extended his right leg and gave it a shake. "Just like new," he said with a wink. "Even better than before."

Dean watched them take their seats, and he stopped for a moment to enjoy the scene before him. He and Cara didn't have a large amount of friends and family, but it was enough to fill the small church.

He looked at them all chatting, smiling and exchanging greetings. Years ago he thought that his family had been torn apart, unlikely to ever recover from the savage brutality that had descended over it. Now he was part of a new family—a family that he knew would rally round in times of need, a family that was aware of his frailties and loved him, anyway.

A gentle hush descended over the congregation, and Dean realized that Cara had arrived. He saw a flurry of activity in the foyer as her bridesmaids adjusted the train on her dress. He caught his breath when her entire profile came into view.

She looked more beautiful than he thought possible,

with a full ivory gown and pearl tiara. He was humbled to see that, through all the finery and splendor, she still wore the plain silver cross around her neck. She had worn it throughout her rehabilitation, pushing herself hard to recover from the injuries that put her in the hospital for six months. For three of those months, she had worn his engagement ring on her left hand, and he had visited every single day, often sleeping overnight in empty hospital beds that the nurses would kindly make up for him.

The pastor stood in front of him with an open Bible, waiting to perform the ceremony. Dean had asked the pastor to use the black Bible that had helped both him and Cara defeat the danger on the mission that had brought them together. Now that same Bible would be used to bind their lives irrevocably together and set them on a new path. The Bible would become their family Bible, symbolizing the promise of God: the promise that came from knowing His blessings were the strongest when your faith was at its weakest.

Dean found himself transfixed by the beauty and poise of his wife-to-be. She caught his gaze and held it, silently mouthing, *"I love you."* He smiled and turned back to the altar to await the first bars of the bridal song, knowing that he would never tire of hearing those words.

Cara had never experienced butterflies like this, not even on the most dangerous missions. This was an altogether new experience for her, and she was tempted to whoop with delight and punch the air. Her mom's presence by her side calmed her joyous spirit and kept her in the moment.

"Cara, honey," she said. "Who will walk you down the aisle?"

Cara's hand flew to her mouth. "Oh, Mom," she said.

"Can you believe that I haven't even thought about it?" She scanned her eyes around the congregation, searching for someone suitable.

Sheila Hanson scurried away and returned with the bemused figure of Colonel Carter Gantry.

"I'm sorry, Colonel," Cara explained, "I forgot to ask someone to walk me down the aisle and I was wondering if you would step into those shoes."

Gantry stepped forward and enveloped her in a hug. "I can only humbly accept the offer to step into the shoes of a man like your father," he said, pulling away. "I never had the honor of meeting him, but I'm sure he would be incredibly proud of you today."

"Thank you, sir," she said, fanning her eyes. "Now stop there before you make me cry and ruin my makeup."

He laughed and changed his tone to a more serious one. "My colleagues at Fort Bliss have informed me that you will be joining their ranks as a sniper trainer. Congratulations, Sergeant Hanson. I know the sniper school will be glad to utilize your remarkable skills."

She nodded. Colonel Gantry knew that the legacy of her injuries prevented her from continuing on active duty, but somehow she hadn't felt sad when the doctors had told her the news. She no longer had the desire to serve overseas, and she didn't feel the overwhelming need to protect those around her at any cost. She wanted to stay close to home and pass on her wealth of knowledge and experience to a new set of snipers, including, she was pleased to see, a fresh batch of female recruits.

The first chords of her entrance music began to play and Colonel Gantry extended his arm, which she took with a smile. As they began the slow walk to the altar, she noticed Gomez smile and give her a thumbs-up. She shook her head, laughing, and averted her gaze to the opposite side of the church where Diane McGovern beamed like a woman who'd won the lottery.

In the midst of it all was the man who would soon be her husband, watching every step bring her closer to him. She looked at his strong, wide shoulders as he stood proudly at the altar. He'd been her savior while she'd recovered in the hospital, always patient, always kind and always tolerant of her anger and frustration. The road to recovery had been a hard one, but God had given her the best possible ally. Dean had taken her out each Sunday so she could attend church, and their discussions of marriage and children had kept her spirits raised even during her darkest times. She knew there were still hard times ahead. The pain and stiffness in her back laid her flat some days, but it was a healing process in more ways than one. God was teaching her to accept her weakness and give the struggle up to Him. God didn't want her to be perfect— He wanted her to be happy.

She reached the altar and turned to give Colonel Gantry a kiss on each cheek. He stepped back and allowed her to take her place by Dean's side. She reached for his hand and he gripped it tightly, running his eyes over her figure, something that still sent shivers through her, head to toe.

"You look beautiful," he whispered.

"I'd rather be in my ghillie suit," she giggled, sending a ripple of laughter through the congregation. She winced and covered her mouth with her hand. "Oops," she whispered, "too loud."

"You ready to be Mrs. McGovern?" he asked, his eyes twinkling.

"I sure am," she replied.

He brought his face close to hers and gave a mischievous smile.

"You up to the job?" he asked, repeating the words he

had said on their very first meeting little more than six months ago—a meeting neither of them had ever envisaged would lead them here.

She played along. "Absolutely, sir."

He kissed her on her nose. "Then let's roll, Sergeant."

* * * * *

Dear Reader,

I hope you enjoyed reading my debut book. I had a great deal of fun writing it. I knew from the get-go that I wanted to write a story to conclude with the words *I will lift up my eyes to the hills. From where shall my help come?* The power of Psalm 121 is strong, speaking to all those who need reassurance that God's protection is always enduring.

Both Dean and Cara are fierce protectors, striving to save each other from danger. They seemed like a good match, both determined to atone for past events and make the world a safer place. But ultimately, it is neither Dean's physical strength nor Cara's rifle that wins the best result in the end—it is the power of prayer. As Cara's life hangs in the balance, Psalm 121 provides the inspiration that both Dean and Cara need to find their way back to each other. And, through prayer, he is able to guide her home.

Thank you for reading my story. I hope it will be the first of many, and I look forward to welcoming you as a reader again.

Elisabeth

Questions for Discussion

1. What was your first impression of Sergeant Cara Hanson? How would you sum up her character?

2. Cara is an elite sniper. Is this a job you think you could do? What are your thoughts on women in combat roles?

3. Captain Dean McGovern was uncertain of allowing Cara into his team. Why do you think he wanted to maintain his distance from her? Do you think he was right to allow her into his all-male team?

4. Dean feels a sense of betrayal after his best friend, Major Christopher Moore, was thought to have joined a terrorist organization. Have you ever experienced disloyalty from a friend? If so, how did it work out in the end?

5. What did you think of Dean McGovern's character? How would you describe him? What effect has his upbringing had on him?

6. Cara is fiercely independent, working alone and trusting in her own judgment. Describe what you think her difficulties might be in becoming part of a close-knit team. Do you think she enjoys working in close proximity with others?

7. Despite losing her father in such a traumatic event, Cara has a strong faith in God, yet Dean's faith waned after the assumed defection of his friend, Chris

Moore. Why did they fare so differently? Why do you think Cara's faith remained strong yet Dean's suffered?

8. Why is Dean so attracted to Cara? What qualities does he see in her that draw him close?

9. When the mission becomes more dangerous, Dean wants Cara to return to base. She refuses. Do you think she should have agreed to Dean's request and returned to base? Why or why not?

10. The Bible verses left for Dean and Cara by Chris Moore are intended to help them in times of need and guide them away from danger. Can you think of any Bible verses that have guided you in times of need?

11. Do you think that Cara changed the dynamic of the team? Would Dean have behaved differently if Cara was not with them? Was her influence a positive one?

12. Do you think it was the right decision for Cara to return to Bear Lake? Did it help her to come to terms with the death of her father?

13. Who or what helps Dean to rekindle his lost faith? Do you think that refinding his faith changes his outlook on life? How so?

14. Did you like the writing style of the author? What, if anything, would you change about the story line?

15. Cara is saved by Dean's prayers. Are there times in your life when you felt prayers being answered? Do you think God answers all prayers?

REQUEST YOUR FREE BOOKS!

2 FREE RIVETING INSPIRATIONAL NOVELS
PLUS 2 FREE MYSTERY GIFTS

Love Inspired.
SUSPENSE

"We used to count the stars at night, Jack. Remember that?"

Oh, he remembered, all right. They'd look skyward and watch each star appear, summer, winter, spring and fall, each season offering its own array, a blend of favorites. Until they'd become distracted by other things. Sweet things.

A sigh welled from somewhere deep within him, a quiet blooming of what could have been. "I remember."

They stared upward, side by side, watching the sunset fade to streaks of lilac and gray. Town lights began to appear north of the bridge, winking on earlier now that it was August. "How long are you here?"

Olivia faltered. "I'm not sure."

He turned to face her, puzzled.

"I'm between lives right now."

He raised an eyebrow, waiting for her to continue. She did, after drawn-out seconds, but didn't look at him. She kept her gaze up and out, watching the tree shadows darken and dim.

"I was married."

He'd heard she'd gotten married several years ago, but the "was" surprised him. He dropped his gaze to her left hand. No ring. No tan line that said a ring had been there this summer. A flicker that might be hope stirred in his chest, but entertaining those notions would get him nothing but trouble, so he blamed the strange feeling on the half-finished sandwich he'd wolfed down on the drive in.

You've eaten fast plenty of times before this and been fine. Just fine.

The reminder made him take a half step forward, just close enough to inhale the scent of sweet vanilla on her hair, her skin.

He shouldn't. He knew that. He knew it even as his hand reached for her hand, the left one bearing no man's ring, and that touch, the press of his fingers on hers, made the tiny flicker inside brighten just a little.

The surroundings, the trees, the thin-lit night and the sound of rushing water made him feel as if anything was possible, and he hadn't felt that way in a very long time. But here, with her?

He did. And it felt good.

Find out what else is going on in Jasper Gulch in HIS MONTANA SWEETHEART by Ruth Logan Herne, available August 2014 from Love Inspired®.

LIEXP0714

Sonya Daniels heard the sharp crack and saw the woman jogging four feet in front of her stumble. Then fall.

Another crack.

Another woman cried out and hit the ground.

"Shooter! Get down! Get down!"

With a burst of horror, Sonya caught on. Someone was shooting at the joggers on the path. Terror froze her for a brief second. A second that saved her life as the bullet whizzed past her head and planted itself in the wooden bench next to her. If she'd been moving forward, she would be dead.

Frantic, she registered the screams of those in the park as she ran full-out, zigzagging her way to the concrete fountain just ahead.

Her only thought was shelter.

A bullet slammed into the dirt behind her and she dropped to roll next to the base of the fountain.

She looked up to find another young woman had beat her there. Terrified brown eyes stared at Sonya and she knew the woman saw her fear reflected back at her. Panting, Sonya listened for more shots.

None came.

And still they waited. Seconds turned into minutes.

"Is it over?" the woman finally whispered. "Is he gone?"

"I don't know," Sonya responded.

Screams still echoed around them. Wails and petrified cries of disbelief.

Sonya lifted her head slightly and looked back at the two women who'd fallen. They still lay on the path behind her.

Sirens sounded.

Sonya took a deep breath and scanned the area across the street. Slowly, she calmed and gained control of her pounding pulse.

Her mind clicked through the shots fired. Two hit the women running in front of her. Her stomach cramped at the thought that she should have been the third victim. She glanced at the bench. The bullet hole stared back. It had dug a groove slanted and angled.

Heart in her throat, Sonya darted to the nearest woman, who lay about ten yards away from her. Expecting a bullet to slam into her at any moment, she felt for a pulse.

When Sonya turns to Detective Brandon Hayes
for help, can he protect her without both of them
losing their hearts?
Pick up HER STOLEN PAST to find out.

Available August 2014
wherever Love Inspired books are sold.

Love Inspired®
SUSPENSE
RIVETING INSPIRATIONAL ROMANCE

Emma Landers has amnesia. Problem is, she can't remember how she got it, why she's injured or why someone wants to hurt her. When she lands on the doorstep of former love Travis Wright, she can barely remember their past history. But she knows she can trust him to protect her. The handsome farmer was heartbroken when Emma left him for the big city. But there's no way he can send her away when gunshots start flying. Now Travis must keep Emma safe while helping her piece together her memories—before it's too late.

A TRACE OF MEMORY
by
VALERIE HANSEN

THE DEFENDERS

Protecting children in need

Available August 2014 wherever
Love Inspired books and ebooks are sold.

LI44613

A reclusive Amish logger, Ethan Gingerich is more comfortable around his draft horses than the orphaned niece and nephews he's taken in. Yet he's determined to provide the children with a good, loving home. The little ones, including a defiant eight-year-old, need a proper nanny. But when Ethan hires shy Amishwoman Clara Barkman, he never expects her temporary position to have such a lasting hold on all of them. Now this man of few words must convince Clara she's found her forever home and family.

BRIDES OF
Amish Country

Finding true love in the land of the Plain People.

The Amish Nanny

by

Patricia Davids

Available August 2014 wherever
Love Inspired books and ebooks are sold.

LI87902